The bedroom door swung open soundlessly and he didn't bother with lights.

Stripping out of his clothes, he slid between the Egyptian cotton sheets and rolled toward the center of his bed. Where he encountered a warm body.

His palm dipped into a nipped-in waist before smoothing over the curve of a hip. Tucker must have hustled to get him this coming-home present. He dipped his head and nuzzled the sweet spot behind the woman's ear.

The next thing he knew, the woman had rolled, tucked her feet into his chest and kicked. Chase flew off the bed and hit the carpeted floor with a soft thud.

"What the hell!" The woman scampered to the other side of the bed and turned on the lamp. "Who are you?"

He stood up, naked and unembarrassed. "I might ask you the same thing, wildcat."

"Oh, my God, you're naked. Get out!"

Before he could move, she nailed him in the chest with a boot. A Western boot. Covered in mud and... He sniffed the air.

"Get out of here, you pervert! I'm calling security."

"Good idea, since I'm throwing you out."

"What? You can't do that."

"Sure I can, kitten. This is my apartment."

Her jaw dropped and then her full lips formed a perfect O.

* * *

Convenient Cowgirl Bride is part of the Red Dirt Royalty series: These Oklahoma millionaires work hard and play harder.

Dear Reader,

Rodeo is a thing. A big thing. It's both a lifestyle and a business. Cowboys and cowgirls who compete on the pro circuit work hard and are on the road almost constantly. There's an order to the rodeos and winning points in order to compete in the big daddy of them all—the Wrangler National Finals Rodeo in Las Vegas. And there are the rodeos that stir the public's imagination: Cheyenne Frontier Days, Calgary Stampede, San Antonio Stock Show and Rodeo, National Western Stock Show and Rodeo in Denver to name a few.

Under normal circumstances, I do a lot of research and make sure places and dates are realistic in my books. In this instance, I admit to fudging Savannah's schedule for the sake of the story. Hopefully, you'll be swept up in the romance and won't begrudge me the poetic license.

I had fun writing this book, revisiting my youth when I trudged out to feed horses no matter the weather, or hooked up the trailer and loaded my horses to head to a rodeo. I was never dedicated enough to make it on the rodeo circuit so I'll admit to living vicariously through Savannah while I wrote her story.

And now that you know my secret, I hope you enjoy Savvi's story, and the love Chase wants to share with her, even if she's a bit more inconveniently convenient than he bargained for.

Happy trails!

Silver James

SILVER JAMES

—

CONVENIENT COWGIRL BRIDE

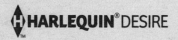

Recycling programs
for this product may
not exist in your area.

ISBN-13: 978-0-373-73490-0

Convenient Cowgirl Bride

Printed in U.S.A.

www.Harlequin.com

Silver James likes walks on the wild side and coffee. Okay. She LOVES coffee. A cowgirl at heart, she's been an army officer's wife and mom, and worked in the legal field, fire service and law enforcement. Now retired from the real world, she lives in Oklahoma, spending her days writing with the assistance of two Newfoundlands, the cat who rules them all and the characters living in her imagination.

Books by Silver James

Harlequin Desire

Red Dirt Royalty

Cowgirls Don't Cry
The Cowgirl's Little Secret
The Boss and His Cowgirl
Convenient Cowgirl Bride

Visit her Author Profile page at Harlequin.com, or silverjames.com, for more titles.

To every reader who is a cowgirl at heart,
to the man who taught me about the soul
of a horse and to the marvelous Harlequin team
who make it easy to let my imagination
gallop across the page.

One

Chasen "Chase" Barron needed a wife like he needed another hangover. Dark thoughts winnowed through his mind as he surveyed his world from the window of his Gulfstream jet. Below him, Las Vegas looked like a necklace of sparkling neon jewels strung on ribbons of car headlights. Vegas never slept. His kind of place.

His latest escapades had landed him back on the front page of the supermarket tabloids—much to his old man's disgust. Chase wasn't a bad guy. Not really. It was just that as head of Barron Entertainment, he was surrounded by beautiful women. And he was definitely a man who enjoyed beautiful women. Frequently. How was he to know the gorgeous actress—who'd told him she was separated—was still very much married to a powerful studio head? Or that she'd invited the paparazzi to record her tryst with Chase in order to… Just thinking about it made his head hurt.

He'd left LA for Nashville to deal with some problems in setting up Barron Entertainment's new country and Western record label, and there were two cute, young singers who wanted an edge. Being seen getting it on with the CEO of Barron Entertainment was their ticket to glory. Who knew those selfies they took would go viral? Yeah, he definitely should have confiscated their cell phones. Water under the bridge now. And lesson learned.

Despite the social media storm, his trip to Nashville had been productive. The new company, Bent Star Records, had launched, making headlines by signing superstar Deacon Tate, and his band, the Sons of Nashville, as the first act. That Deke was Chase's cousin was beside the point. Family did business with family. Which brought him back around to the situation at hand.

Waking up, predictably hungover, to his father's edict to marry the very disagreeable daughter of a business associate, Chase figured there was only one way out—head back to Las Vegas with all speed and ignore his father's demands. Besides, the old man hadn't called in his brothers for a family intervention, right? Or maybe dear old Dad was finally getting the message now that Chance, Cord and Clay had all defied the old jackass, married the women they loved and were living the lives they wanted without his permission.

Chase admired his older brothers. He'd fallen in with the old man's edicts during the family confrontations, but had secretly rooted for his siblings. Now if he could just figure out what was going on with his identical twin. Cash had been a coiled snake ready to strike every time Chase had seen him lately. And he was worried. They used to be so close they knew what the other was thinking. Not anymore.

But solving the mystery of his twin's behavior would have to wait. Chase had his own problems— mainly figuring out how not to get engaged to Janiece Carroll. While pretty enough, courtesy of a personal trainer and a skilled plastic surgeon, Janiece was High Maintenance, capitalized and trademarked. The former debutante had a voice like nails on a blackboard and the social skills of a spoiled toddler. Yeah, he needed to figure out a way to dodge this particular bullet.

On the ground, he traded the jet for his Jaguar F-type convertible. Once the top was down, he cranked up the sound system and the strains of Deacon's newest hit, "Heading Home," filled the hangar. He pulled out, maneuvered off airport property and headed into Las Vegas proper. The dazzling array of lights and throngs of people on the Strip felt like home.

Downshifting the powerful Jag, he coasted to a stop at a traffic light. Two women in spangly mini-dresses barely covering their butts sauntered by in the crosswalk in front of him. They watched him, their invitation plain in their expressions. Part of him was tempted. Part of him wanted only to hit his bed in the penthouse apartment at the Barron Crown Hotel and Casino. The light changed and the opportunity was lost. He wasn't disappointed. He'd had enough female manipulation for a while.

Chase cruised down the street debating whether to pull into the main entrance of the hotel or head around the block to the employees' parking garage. He hadn't shaken the headache so he decided to forgo the casino's clamor. The guard on duty at the garage nodded to him and opened the gate with a quiet "Good to have you back, sir."

After parking in his spot near the private elevators, he snagged his satchel and overnight bag. Having semipermanent residences in both LA and Nashville made for light travel. He rubbed his jaw as he rode up in the elevator.

Cash had upgraded security and it took Chase's thumbprint to get to any of the secured floors, including the top floor, where he resided. His card key was in his hand when he stepped into the beautifully appointed foyer. His apartment took up a third of the floor. Three suites—the smallest and cheapest going for ten grand a night—occupied the rest of the space.

Everything about the Crown was five-star, including his apartment. He card-keyed the door and stepped inside, as soft lights slowly brightened. Motion detectors meant he never walked into a darkened room— except the master bedroom. The light switch in there was the old-fashioned kind.

He moved into the open living area and hit the wet bar. He skipped the bottles of top-shelf liquor and grabbed a cold bottle of beer from the fridge instead. Mail was stacked on his desk and he checked it with a bored eye. His vice president of operations would have already handled anything important. Tucker was his cousin and he trusted the man implicitly—again, it was that whole family-doing-business-together thing.

Wandering into the gourmet kitchen, Chase tried to decide if he was hungry. A plastic-wrapped tray of meat, cheese and a variety of artisan breads occupied one shelf in the Sub-Zero refrigerator. His pilot would have alerted Tuck of their pending arrival, and as usual, his cousin had taken care of him before shutting down for the night. The tray was perfect. He slid it out onto the granite top of the breakfast bar and hitched a hip onto the wrought iron bar stool. He ate and drank, watching the play of lights outside the floor-to-ceiling windows bracketing the living space.

A few minutes might have passed, or a few hours. He wasn't sure and didn't care. His headache had receded and he finally felt drowsy. He covered the tray and shoved it back into the fridge. As he stepped into the hallway leading to his bedroom, the lights behind him faded while the sconces in the hall flickered on. He'd left his briefcase at his desk and his overnight bag in the hallway. Housekeeping would deal with it in the morning, after he went to his business office on the third floor.

It was only one in the morning. He should have been fired up to hit the casino floor, or to check out one of the shows playing at the hotel. He should have hit his office, but he was tired. That fact might have worried him but he was too tired—or too bored—to care.

The bedroom door swung open soundlessly and he didn't bother with lights. He could navigate this room in the dark. After stripping out of his clothes, he slid between the 1200-thread-count Egyptian cotton sheets and rolled toward the center of the bed.

Where he encountered a warm body.

Reaching out, he found the soft cotton of a T-shirt. Chase wondered briefly if it was one of his. His palm dipped into a nipped-in waist before smoothing over the curve of a hip and down to the bare skin of a mus-

cular thigh. Tucker must have hustled to get him this
coming-home present. He dipped his head and nuzzled
the sweet spot behind the woman's ear as his hand
cupped her full breast.

The next thing he knew, the woman raked her nails
down his arm, rolled, tucked her feet into his chest and
kicked. Chase flew off the bed and hit the carpeted
floor with a soft thud.

"What the hell!" The woman scampered to the other
side of the bed and hit the on button for the lamp on
the nightstand. "Who are you?"

He stood up, naked and unembarrassed. She was in
his bed in his apartment in his hotel. He had nothing
to be embarrassed about. "I might ask you the same
thing, wildcat."

"Oh, my God, you're naked. Get out!"

Before he could move, she nailed him in the chest
with a boot. A Western boot. Covered in mud and…
he sniffed the air. Bending, he snatched the boot and
stared at it, barely ducking in time when a second boot
sailed toward his face.

"Get out of here, you pervert!" She snatched the
phone and began dialing. "I'm calling Security."

"Good idea, since I'm throwing you out."

"What? You can't do that."

"Sure I can, kitten. This is my apartment."

Her jaw dropped and then her full lips formed a perfect O. Chase liked the looks of that. And it showed.
Her eyes dropped and she flushed before tilting her
chin to face him eye to eye. She stood on the far side
of the bed and he got a good look at her.

She wasn't too tall—maybe five-six or five-seven—
and while the baggy T-shirt covered most of her attri-

butes, he could scope out her legs—long and muscular. Then he caught the saying emblazoned on her shirt: Sometimes A Cowgirl Has To Do What A Cowboy Can't. Reading the message stretched across her chest didn't help calm his libido. He dragged his gaze to her face, which was surrounded by a thick curtain of black hair, sleep tousled and begging for a man to run his fingers through it. Brown eyes bored into him from behind thick lashes that swept her high cheekbones with each blink.

"You're one of the Barrons," she murmured, her eyes still fastened on his face. Her tongue darted out from between her lips and he had to bite back a groan. "Can you, uh, put on some pants or something?"

He turned and walked to the chair where he'd dropped his jeans. Stepping into them commando, Chase glanced over his shoulder, only to catch her staring at his butt. His libido immediately whispered sweet nothings in his ear, but he'd already been burned twice in the past month. That shut up his libido and his body calmed down immediately.

"You wanna explain why you're in my bed?"

"I'm Savannah Wolfe."

She said it as though he should know the name. He didn't. "Yeah, and?"

"I… I have permission to be here. Kade—"

"No one has permission to be here."

"But—" Her face flushed as her temper flared. Chase discovered he liked putting that color in her cheeks.

"No one, wildcat, especially not you."

"Stop calling me that."

He showed her the four red marks on the inside

of his forearm. "I think it fits. However, as much as I'd like to play, you're not staying. Get your stuff and get out."

"But—"

"We can do this like civilized people or I can call Security and have you arrested for trespassing."

"But—"

He pulled his cell from his hip pocket. "Tired of the *but*s, cat."

"I—"

He hit a button and she dropped her gaze.

"Fine. Get out so I can get dressed."

"Not happenin', girl." He snagged her boots and tossed them to her. She caught them easily.

"Fine. If you get off on watchin', then you are a big ol' pervert." She strode over to another chair and grabbed her jeans and a plaid shirt. An old canvas duffel bag slouched on the floor next to the chair. She had her shirt on but not buttoned and one leg in her jeans when Security hit the doorway.

"Problem, Mr. Barron?"

"Not anymore. Please escort this woman off the premises."

The dark-suited security officer didn't give Savannah a chance to get dressed. He snagged her bag, draped it over her shoulder, grabbed her boots and jammed them into her chest, gripped her arm and frog-marched her out. Sputtering and cussing, the girl did her best to get her jeans on. Chase followed them to the door and out into the foyer. He was grinning in the face of her scowl as the elevator doors closed. Pink polka-dotted panties. Now that was a sight he wouldn't forget any time soon.

Two

Savannah had never been so mortified in her life. She was going to kill Kaden Waite the next time she saw him.

"Chase is in Nashville until after the rodeo," Kade had told her, knowing money was tight and she'd probably be sleeping in her truck or in Indigo's stall. "No one will be there. I'll call the hotel and set it up."

He had. She'd checked in that night with no problem. The desk clerk had barely looked at her. Either Chase Barron had strange women asking for his card key all the time or Kade had totally smoothed the way. Before her ignominious exit, things had been great. She'd gotten Indigo settled into his stall at the Clark County Fairgrounds and had enough grain left to feed him well. She'd unhooked her horse trailer and parked it in the designated area near the barn before driving to the Strip.

She'd found a place in the Crown Hotel and Casino's parking lot and locked up her old truck. Not that it would take more than a twist of baling wire to pop the locks. Even with the odometer logging 200,000 miles, the old Ford still got her from rodeo to rodeo. She even had half a tank of gas—hopefully enough to last until she won the barrel event that weekend. And she had to win. She had a total of $175.00 in her checking account and twenty bucks in her pocket.

Then she'd woken up to a strange man in bed with her. The man who lived in that penthouse suite. Chase Barron. All six-plus feet of sexy male with his lean, I-run-on-the-treadmill-every-day body, his silky dark hair and those coffee-colored eyes. She jerked her thoughts back and remembered she'd nailed him in the chest with her boot. He deserved it. He was the world's biggest jerk.

The security guy mostly ignored her, but the walls of the elevator were polished to the point they might as well have been mirrors. She struggled into her jeans, got them buttoned and her belt buckled. He didn't give her time to dig a pair of socks out of her duffel. Marching her barefoot across the lobby to the obvious entertainment of everyone they encountered just added to her now miserable night.

Security shoved her through the entrance, held open by a smirking doorman. Savannah stumbled a few steps, found her balance and moved to a granite planter. Plopping her butt on the edge of it, she glared at the man standing over her, ready to snatch her up to keep her moving. "Hold your frickin' horses, dude. I'm putting on my socks and boots."

It took her a minute to stamp her boots on. Straightening to her full height, chin up, she offered him her glaringest glare. "I can find my way out."

Turning on her heel, head still high, she stomped across the valet drive and headed into the crowded lot. Her truck was parked in the far corner. She kept walking, and about three rows in, her escort dropped back, then stopped altogether. She ducked behind an RV, and when she peeked back, he was returning to the hotel.

Still seething, she found her truck, only to discover the front tire was flat. That made her choice easy. Rather than driving back to the fairgrounds to sleep in Indy's stall, she'd sleep in the truck. She was too tired to change the tire tonight. Crawling inside, she swiped at her cheeks. She didn't have the spare time or energy to waste on tears. She *would* be back here in Las Vegas come December, competing in the Wrangler National Finals Rodeo, but that meant she had to be at her best for this week's qualifying rodeo. February was a late start but she was determined.

She pushed her duffel against the passenger door, stretched across the bench seat and jerked the Indian blanket off the back of the seat to cover her legs. She would deal with everything in the morning, including calling Mr. Kaden "I'll fix it" Waite to tell him not to do her any more favors.

Savannah sat straight up, cussing. She couldn't call Kade. She couldn't call anyone. Her phone was plugged in, charging on the nightstand, next to the bed belonging to the jackass who lived on the fiftieth floor of the monster hotel looming just beyond her windshield.

Dammit. She would have to face the man again in the morning. With her luck, the jerk face would just throw her phone away when he found it, which would suck because she didn't have the money to get a new one.

Snatching a baseball cap off the headache rack behind the seat, she put it on and pulled the bill over her eyes. She had to sleep or she'd be sluggish tomorrow. She needed to work Indy in the arena because he'd been off training for three weeks. Her horse needed to settle and be in shape to get a good time for the first round. If her time wasn't fast enough, there wouldn't be a second round and she'd be in a world of economic hurt. She was already two rodeos behind on getting points and winnings.

Savvie thumped her duffel and sought a more comfortable position. She eventually drifted off.

Just before dawn, Chase found the woman's phone, when it buzzed on his nightstand. Irritated, he rolled over and grabbed it, ready to throw it against the far wall until he saw Kaden calling on the screen. It was the ranch manager of the Crown B. Curious, he answered.

"Yeah?"

"Uh…is Savannah around?"

"No."

"Where is she?"

"Why do you want to know?"

"Who is this?"

"Chase Barron."

Silence stretched for a long moment before Kade replied. "Chase? Kaden Waite. I thought you were in Nashville."

"I was until last night. Found someone in my bed, Kade."

"Damn. I'm sorry. Chance and Cord told me it'd be all right if Savvie stayed in your place while you were gone. They expected you to be in Nashville for at least another two weeks. The rodeo is over Saturday night and Sav would be back on the road Sunday."

"She your girlfriend?" Chase didn't expect the burst of laughter from the other man.

"Kissing her would be like kissing my sister. Our mothers were tight and we grew up practically next door to each other."

"So she's Chickasaw?" That would help explain the sleek, black hair, carved cheekbones and snapping brown eyes.

"Nope. Choctaw. Is that a problem?" Kade's voice took on an edge. "Look, Chase, I was trying to help the kid out. She's living on a shoestring and has big dreams about being the next All-Around Cowgirl. She was gonna sleep in her truck or her horse's stall, so I figured since you were gone and your brothers said—"

"Yeah, yeah. I rained on her parade by coming home early. Not a big deal, Kade. Look, she's out right now. Forgot her phone. I'll have her call you." Chase was lying through his teeth. He wasn't about to explain he'd kicked her out last night.

"That's okay. She'll just get pissed because I'm checking up on her. I worry about her being out there alone, ya know?"

"Gotcha. Anything else? I gotta go, man." Yeah, he had to go find her before Kade found out.

"Thanks, Chase."

"Anytime, bro." And that last slipped out before he

could catch it. Luckily, Kade hung up without comment. Chase was convinced Kade was a product of one of the old man's liaisons. The guy didn't act like he had a clue and he always kept an employer-employee barrier up between him and the Barron boys. Still, they all had their suspicions.

At the moment, though, figuring out Kade's parentage was less pressing than finding the girl Chase had tossed out like yesterday's garbage. He realized, belatedly, that she'd tried to explain her presence, and he never gave her the chance. Plus, he'd forced her into a walk of shame with Security—with everyone in the lobby there to witness every step. He could be a right bastard sometimes. He called Tucker about sending someone to the fairgrounds later to locate Savannah, and arranging a comped room for the girl.

A shower and a cup of coffee later, Chase dressed in an impeccable suit and custom black boots, then stood staring out the window. Activity in the parking lot below drew his attention. Red and blue flashing lights. Police. Members of hotel security. And a beat-up old truck. He slammed his mug on the counter and headed to the door at a trot.

Downstairs, the doorman got the heavy glass door open half a second before Chase would have slammed it open himself. He ignored the valet and strode into the parking lot. As he approached the knot of cops and security personnel, he heard the woman's indignant voice.

"But I wasn't soliciting that dude. He came on to me!" Her fisted hands hung stiffly at her sides and she had a smear of grease across one cheek. "I was just changing my tire."

Chase noticed the jack, the flat tire and the sorry state of the old Ford truck in general. Kade hadn't lied about her circumstances. And now that Chase wasn't pissed off and worried he was being set up again, he realized how gorgeous she looked, even in the same faded T-shirt from last night. She also had on a plaid shirt, faded jeans, muddy boots, and her face was dirty. She barely kept her temper in check, and Chase had the insane desire to find out what would happen when she snapped. Instead, he pushed into the group.

"I see you're still here, Miss Wolfe."

She glared, and he had to bite back a smile.

"You know her, boss?" Bart Stevens, head of hotel security, stepped up beside him.

"Kade called this morning," Chase said to her, without answering his security chief's question. He held out her phone. "You left this behind last night."

Savannah stared at him but didn't reach for the phone. Her expression reminded him of Miz Beth, the woman who'd helped raise the Barron brothers, staring at a rattlesnake—as if she didn't know whether to be afraid or take a hoe to his neck. He stepped closer, unsnapped the flap on the pocket over her left breast and slipped the phone inside. Turning to Stevens, he added, "Call the garage and have them send someone over to change the tire and move the truck."

"I can change my own tire," she growled at him, and he was reminded again of her wildcat tendencies.

"I'm sure you can, Savannah. But I'm paying people to change tires whether they are changing them or sitting on their butts. Grab your stuff and come with me."

"No." Her fists were now planted on her hips, her

face darkening as her eyes narrowed. "Don't do me any favors, Mr. Barron."

Oh, yeah, this was going to be fun. "Do you really want to do this in front of an audience?" He gestured toward the three uniformed security guards, his suited security chief and the four LVPD officers circling them.

"No. I just want to change my flat, get in my truck and get to the fairgrounds so I can work my horse."

"While the hotel garage is servicing your truck, I'll take you to the fairgrounds and you can work your horse."

Savannah glanced around before she stepped close to him and snarled into his ear. "Why are you being nice? You threw me out on my ass last night."

"I apologize." He said it quietly, his gaze covering the other men. "Long story. I'll explain later." He stepped back and said more loudly, "C'mon, Savannah, I'll buy you breakfast and then we'll head out to Clark County."

He offered his most appealing smile, the one most women begged to get. This woman just rolled her eyes, pivoted and reached into her truck to grab the duffel. She jerked her keys from her front pocket and dangled them from her fingers. Chase nodded to one of the guards to take the keys. A second guard reached for the duffel. Savannah relinquished it after a short tussle.

"I can carry my own stuff," she muttered.

"Yes, but this is my hotel and guests don't carry their own luggage."

She arched a brow at Chase. "Guest?"

"Come back to my apartment for breakfast and we'll talk."

Her gaze raked over him from his face to his boots and back to his eyes. "You don't impress me as a man who talks much, unless he's issuing orders."

Chase threw back his head and laughed. He dropped his arm across her shoulders and drew her along with him. "You think you have my number, wildcat. C'mon." When they had a modicum of privacy, he lowered his head closer to hers. "You can grab a hot shower and clean clothes while we're waiting for room service."

"Your bathroom better have a lock on the door."

He snorted and another deep belly laugh erupted as he squeezed her in a side hug. She tensed and tried to lean away, but he didn't let her. "I promise to be on my best behavior. Besides, Kade would probably beat me up if I tried anything."

The tension left her body. "You really did talk to him?"

"Yeah." He didn't say anything else until they crossed the lobby and entered the penthouse elevator. Chase took her duffel from the guard and the doors closed behind them. "I'm sorry I jumped the gun and didn't let you explain. I was coming off a situation that had to do with two girls and some selfies posted to social media and subsequently picked up by the press. That's why I came back to Vegas early. I also bypassed the front desk coming in, so they didn't have a chance to tell me I had a guest."

She turned her head and her lips quirked. A flash of heat washed over him as he watched her mouth. She stiffened beside him almost as if she'd read his mind. He needed to work on his poker face. Chase blinked to break the connection growing between them. She was a beautiful woman, sexy in a blunt, earthy way, and totally unlike his usual side dish. Still, the attraction remained—an attraction he wanted to explore. She'd be in town only a week. That was more than enough time.

Three

Chase leaned on the metal railing of the outdoor arena fence and watched Savannah ride the big black horse. The gelding loped around the perimeter, a rocking-chair gait that made the rider's hips undulate in a way that every part of Chase stood up and noticed. He'd grown up around horses, and cattle, but nothing had ever turned him on like watching Savannah simply ride in circles. Which was completely crazy. He wasn't a cowboy. He'd never hit the rodeo circuit like Cord and Chance, or Cash for that matter. He could ride. He'd grown up on the Crown B. But this? He shifted uncomfortably, and jerked when his phone buzzed in his hip pocket.

Tucker. Chase swiped his thumb across the phone to answer. "Yeah, bud. What's up?"

"I have her booked into a room with full comp."

"Thanks."

"You wanna explain what's going on?"

He would if he understood it himself. Instead, he went for the easy answer. "She's a friend of Kade's."

"A…friend."

"Get your mind out of the gutter, Tuck. Not that kind of friend. They grew up together, sort of like brother and sister. She's here for the rodeo this weekend. I'm doing him a favor."

"Uh-huh."

Silence stretched between them before Chase finally broke it. "Say what's on your mind, Tuck."

"I got a look at the security footage, man."

"Ah."

"Yeah. The video has been deleted." The uncomfortable silence returned, but Tucker sliced through it this time. "She's not a stray dog, Chase. You can't toss her out, then leave food on the porch."

Chase thought fast because after talking to Kade, he did feel sorry he'd thrown her out, but there was something more—something he couldn't quite put his finger on. "If I'd known who she was, Tuck, I would have comped her a room last night. She's not a stray. She's Kade's friend."

"Whatever, cuz." Voices hummed in the background before Tuck continued. "When are you coming back?"

"What's up?"

"Not sure. Security thinks there might be something hinky going on out on the floor."

"Keep them on it. I'll be back after lunch."

"Okay."

He continued to silently watch Savannah exercise

her horse, but when he noticed the animal's gait was off, he started to say something. She'd already realized there was a problem, reining the animal to a stop and slipping off his back. She checked his rear leg, then walked him to the gate. Chase met her there and took in her slumped shoulders and tight expression with one sweep of his gaze as he opened it for her.

"What's wrong?"

"Indy was kicked three weeks ago. I dropped out of that rodeo and didn't enter another to give him a chance to heal up. He seemed fine when we got here so I paid my entry. If I don't run him, I lose the fee."

"What's the vet say?"

She mumbled something Chase couldn't understand, so he touched her shoulder. Her muscles twitched but she didn't jerk away. "Savannah?"

"I don't have the money for a vet." She wouldn't meet his gaze, keeping her chin tucked in and her eyes downcast. "It's just a deep muscle bruise. I had someone look at it. Rest, heat, mild exercise."

"But…"

She pulled away from him and began leading the horse toward the long barn with the rental stalls. "But nothing. If he can't run, my season is over. I can't afford to buy another horse as good as Indy. Thing is, I have to win to keep going. I don't even know if I can get him back to Oklahoma and keep him long enough to heal. Grain isn't cheap." Snapping her mouth shut, she tucked her chin against her chest again. "I'm sorry. I didn't mean to dump my problems on you. It's none of your business. I'll deal with it." She moved away from him, putting the big horse between them when she added, "I need to cool Indy down, muck his stall and brush him. Can you stick around to give me a ride back to pick up my truck?"

"Yeah, I can do that."

When they entered the barn, and he figured out which stall was hers, Chase sent her off to cool down the horse. He took off his bespoke suit coat, stripped off his designer tie and rolled up his sleeves. Before he grabbed the shovel and hay fork, he placed a call to Tuck to get the best large-animal vet in Vegas to the fairgrounds to check out Savannah's horse.

While Chase shoveled manure out of the stall, then raked the dirt and clean straw into place, his internal dialogue was short and sarcastic. He didn't need to get wrapped up in this girl's problems. Not his style. At all. But her tough-girl exterior and the flashes of vulnerability he glimpsed stirred something deep inside—something more than his libido.

Chase knew better than to examine that feeling too closely. He wasn't a white knight and this girl didn't need him riding to her rescue. Her clothes were old, her boots scuffed and run-down at the heels, her tack fixed so many times the repairs had repairs. She needed more than a quick roll in the hay and that was his standard operating procedure. He was definitely a love 'em and leave 'em kind of guy. Plus, he preferred his women sleek, designer and aware of the rules of his game. He didn't want—and definitely didn't need—a down-home cowgirl next door like Savannah Wolfe.

By the time Savannah returned with Indigo, Chase had bought fresh alfalfa hay and a bag of grain and filled the stall's manger and feed bucket.

He'd learned long ago it was better to ask for forgiveness than to ask for permission. Far fewer arguments that way. But he didn't quite manage to get her off the property before the vet showed up. They had that argument while the doctor examined her horse. When he delivered his prognosis—a deep muscle bruise, possibly bone chipping—all the fight went out of her. And Chase's heart went out to her—a wholly unexpected, and unusual, feeling.

Savannah didn't argue when he led her to his Jag. She looked defeated as he settled her into the passenger seat. He got behind the wheel and glanced at her before putting the sleek car into gear and driving off. "I'm sorry, Savannah. Indy will recover, though. That's good, right?"

"Yeah." She wouldn't look at him, and her flat tone didn't make him feel better.

They rode in silence for several miles. Savannah inhaled deeply and straightened her shoulders. She opened her mouth to speak, but the ringing of his phone interrupted. He hit the answer button on the steering wheel.

"Chase Barron."

"Where are you, Chase?"

"We're driving back to the hotel, Tuck. What's up?" He didn't like the tight sound of his cousin's voice.

"You need to pull over and take me off Bluetooth."

"Okay." He located a convenience store up ahead and pulled in. With a few deft motions, he disconnected the phone function and held his cell next to his ear. "Talk to me."

"I just got a request to free up two of the suites on the penthouse floor. For Uncle Cyrus and the Carrolls—father and daughter."

Chase glanced at Savannah, who was pretending

she wasn't eavesdropping, not that she had a choice in the close confines of the sports car. "When?"

"They're arriving Friday." Tucker cleared his throat on a choked chortle. "I'm not supposed to tell you. Your old man is planning to ambush you."

"Ha. Thanks for the heads-up."

"What are you going to do?"

He cut his eyes to the passenger seat, an idea starting to form in his brain. A really bad idea. Or one that was utterly brilliant. Chase couldn't decide. "Not sure yet. I'll let you know."

Disconnecting the call, he put the Jag in gear and pulled back out into traffic. For the entire ride, until he turned into the valet lane at the Crown, he didn't give Savannah a chance to question him. With his hand gripping her arm just above the elbow, he guided her inside and to the VIP clerk at check-in to get a card key. In the private elevator, he punched in the number for her floor.

"We've comped you a room, and your things are already there. Grab a shower and clean clothes, then buzz me at extension seven star star one. I'll come down to get you, and we'll go back up to the apartment. We'll decide on lunch and order."

"Mr. Barron—"

"Chase. Please, Savannah? Just do this for me. We'll figure out something about your situation, okay?"

"Okay." The doors slithered open silently and she stepped out. He leaned against the panel, keeping the elevator open. "It'll be okay, Savannah."

She tilted her head and watched him through unblinking eyes. "Why are you being nice to me?"

The corner of his mouth quirked into a sardonic

smile before he could stop himself. "I have no idea. I just know that I want to." He freed the door and it closed on her bemused expression.

Upstairs, he paced through the apartment, fitting pieces of a plan together. He had a crap ton of stuff to do and very little time to do it in.

Forty-five minutes later, he had a handle on almost everything. All he needed now was Savannah's cooperation. Considering the deal he'd put together, he figured it wouldn't be too hard to win her over, despite misgivings expressed by his brother Chance, and by Kade.

Savannah stood under the hot water pouring from the rainfall showerhead. Her room was like a little minisuite. There was a sitting area with a huge LED TV, and a small table for two next to the window that looked out over the Strip. The mattress on the king-size bed bounced her a little when she flopped on it, and then sucked her into its memory-foam goodness. The bathroom was…huge, sporting a whirlpool garden tub big enough for two and a separate granite-walled shower big enough for even more.

She pressed her hands against the stone wall and bowed her head. If some tears mixed in with the water, who would know? Besides her. She didn't cry. Didn't have the time or the inclination for it. But here she was, bawling twice in less than twenty-four hours. Letting go of a dream was hard, but she had no choice.

Indigo was hurt too badly to race. In fact, the vet had wanted to take him to the clinic for X-rays. Her horse was done. Out for at least three months, if not forever. The whole thing was so stupid. She'd been mounted, waiting her turn to run at a rodeo last month in Denver. Another competitor had ridden up beside her and within seconds, the other horse had freaked, whirled and nailed poor Indigo in the gaskin, the area between the thigh and hock. She'd checked Indy, but there was no broken skin. Thinking the flighty horse had missed, she'd run the barrels that night and Indy pulled up lame at the end of the run.

Guilt swamped her. One of the guys with the rodeo stock company had looked at Indy for her. He knew almost as much as a vet and had diagnosed a deep bruise. He'd recommended rest. Hot packs. Then alternate hot and cold packs. She didn't have money for a vet and she darn sure wasn't going to call home for a bailout. Her mother and Tom, Mom's latest loser boyfriend, would be all up in her face with the I-told-you-so's. Well, they'd told her so, and now she had no choice but to tuck her tail between her legs and sneak home. Her shoulders shook as she cried harder.

Maybe Kade would loan her enough money to get back to Oklahoma, though she didn't know what she'd do once she got there. Surely some of the restaurants or clubs in Oklahoma City were hiring. She'd need good tips to pay Kade back. She'd have to sell Indy. She couldn't afford to board him—or get him properly doctored by a vet—and with Tom living with her mom, she couldn't stay at the farm.

The thought of losing her horse hurt her heart. The first time she'd put him through his paces she knew she had a winner, and it had revived her dream of becoming the Champion All-Around Cowgirl at the Wrangler National Finals Rodeo.

And now that dream was dead, ground into the red dirt she'd never be able to shake off her boots.

Savannah twirled the shower handle and the water flow stopped. Braiding her hair while it was still wet, she didn't bother with makeup—not that she often wore any—and pulled on a pair of clean jeans, her boots and a T-shirt. She didn't want to see Chase Barron, sit in the same room with him, have lunch with him. Chase knew too much, saw too much. And with his dark hair, coffee-colored eyes and dimpled grin, he was far too dangerous for her to deal with when she was feeling this vulnerable.

Still, she picked up the phone and dialed his extension. While he'd been a major jerk in the beginning, he had stepped up to help when no one else had. Not that she needed help. She was just fine on her own—had proved that since she was twelve, when her mother brought that first scumbag home and he'd tried to get into bed with Savannah. She'd handled everything life had thrown at her so far. She would handle this, too. Because she had no choice.

When his phone beeped to announce Savannah was waiting, Chase was as ready as he could be. He went down in the elevator to retrieve her. Over hamburgers—her choice for lunch—he laid out his plan.

"I want to sponsor you."

She choked, grabbed the glass of expensive spring water he'd poured for her and chugged it. "Excuse me?" she sputtered once she could talk.

"You want to go to the National Finals, right?"

She nodded but didn't speak.

"I know Indigo is out of commission for now. I

know you're on your last dime, almost literally. I know that piece-of-shit truck won't make another thousand miles, much less the ten thousand you'll need to drive to hit enough rodeos to qualify for Nationals."

Savannah just watched him, brow knitted, lips pursed. He really wanted to kiss those lips. Which was crazy, given what he was about to propose. When silence stretched between them, he pulled his eyes away from her mouth and refocused on her eyes.

"I'll sponsor you. Well, technically, Barron Entertainment will. The company will provide you with a new truck, a new trailer—both carrying our name. I've talked to Kade about a replacement horse. He has one in mind and can have it here before the first round Friday night. I'll pay your gas, all other travel expenses, entry fees, insurance, stall rentals and whatever rodeo-related expenses you have."

Her tongue darted out to wet her lips, her eyes wide now, and unbelieving. He wanted to chase her tongue with his lips. That could wait. He had to win her over to his plan first. "After Nationals, win, lose or draw, I'll pay you a bonus of two hundred and fifty thousand dollars."

"There has to be catch."

His little wildcat didn't trust easily. That was okay. He had every expectation he could convince her this was all to her benefit.

"What, besides barrel racing, do I have to do to receive this Barron bounty?"

"Marry me."

Four

"Marry you." Her voice was flat to her own ears, though she all but screeched her next question. "Are you out of your frickin' mind?"

"Maybe."

Savannah stared at Chase, wondering what bizarre thing would come out of his mouth next. "You're crazy. I'm not going to marry you. I… You…" She breathed through the tightness in her chest. He'd dangled her dream in front of her only to jerk it out of her reach. "No. You're completely nuts. Less than twenty-four hours ago you had Security perp walk me out of this hotel. Now you're all…" She fluttered her hands, at a loss for how to describe his actions. "Crazy. Just crazy."

"Please hear me out, Savannah."

She folded her arms across her chest, leaned back in

the very comfortable chair and cocked a brow. "Fine. I'm listening."

"I find I'm in need of a wife."

"Uh-huh."

"A wife of my choosing, not my father's."

She leaned forward, curious despite her misgivings. This explanation was going to be a doozy.

"I'm fairly certain you're aware of my…reputation."

The snort escaped before she could hold it back. "Reputation? What? You mean the one that lands you on the front cover of every tabloid from LA to London? A different woman in your bed every night? Or do you mean the sex tapes floating around the internet? Yeah. I think the whole world is aware of your *reputation*, Mr. Barron."

He attempted to look contrite but she didn't buy it for a second.

"Call me Chase, please." He brushed a manicured hand through his expertly styled hair. "Look, Savannah, this is a win-win for you. And for me."

"You still haven't explained your reasons, Chase."

"My father has decided I need to settle down, and I need to get married in order to do that."

"So why me?"

"Because he has an acceptable wife picked out for me already."

She couldn't breathe for a moment, and her voice sounded slightly strangled as she pushed out words she didn't want to say. "An *acceptable* wife. And I'm not. You want to marry me because I'm a dirt-poor, Choctaw cowgirl and it will piss your old man off." Heat surged in her cheeks and her fingers tingled from adrenaline. She wanted to hit him. Or run. Anything but sit here and be embarrassed by this rich clown.

"No, Savannah. That's not true. Not really. Yes, I need to be legally married before he gets here Friday. Yes, you happen to be here and in a position where we can help each other out. But no, it didn't occur to me that you're…that you would be something to taunt him with. Well, beyond the fact that I'd be preemptively marrying you before he could try to force me to marry Janiece."

He sank onto the granite block that served as a coffee table, scrubbing at his face with the palms of his hands—hands, she reminded herself, with a better manicure than her own. There he sat in designer slacks, a starched cotton shirt with so many threads she probably couldn't count that high, his high-dollar haircut and boots that likely cost more than she'd made last year. And here she sat in faded jeans fraying at the back pockets, scuffed boots all but falling apart, a T-shirt advertising a boot company, and her hair semi-tamed into a braid.

"But I have to be honest, now that you've brought it to my attention. Yes, if you marry me, there will be flack. From the old man and probably from my family. I've already talked to my brother Chance. He's an attorney. I want him to draw up a prenuptial agreement."

She opened her mouth to protest, but Chase held up a hand to stay her argument.

"It's to protect you as much as me. I'm making certain promises to you. You have every expectation that I'll deliver. The prenup ensures that you'll be taken care of, as promised. I won't lie. Chance is not happy with me, but that's par for the course. I'm sort of the bad seed in the family." He offered a boyish grin meant to disarm her, and it succeeded—to a point.

"I'm not your type, Chase." She tried to meet his gaze head-on and add a glower, but she couldn't keep her eyes from sliding to the side as she spoke the truth. "I'm rough. I live from payday to payday. I don't wear heels or designer duds. I don't talk like you. Heck, I bet your hands are softer than mine. No one is going to buy this marriage as anything other than what it is—a marriage of convenience to get you out of trouble with your father."

Chase couldn't deny her words, nor would he do her the disservice of trying. She told the truth, but at the same time, there was something compelling about that. Most women—okay, every woman he'd ever dated—wanted something from him and would tell him whatever they thought he wanted to hear in order to get it. Savannah was different. She was... real. What he saw was what he'd get. And what he saw fascinated him.

She was prickly, stubborn, full of pride, curvy, tomboyish—all the things he stayed away from when it came to women. She'd be way more trouble than she was worth. She'd be a crimp in his social life. She'd bedevil him like crazy. And some perverse part of him looked forward to the challenge, actually craved it. He watched her struggle to meet his eyes, realized she was feeling exposed and didn't like the feeling.

Despite his social failings where the opposite sex was concerned, Chase understood people and their motivations on a visceral level. That made him extremely successful in the entertainment business. He sensed this woman would always speak the truth, at least as she perceived it. He'd appreciate that in the long run, if not always in the present. And despite her strength, there was a vulnerability shrouding her that stirred a deeply buried protective streak.

"I won't embarrass you, Savannah. I wouldn't do that to you. I'll take care of you for the length of the contract between us. You'll walk away at the end with what I've promised—new truck, the trailer, the horse we get from Kade, all your expenses. Clothes. Food. Hotels. Vets for the horse, including Indigo. I'll get Kade to bring your new horse out and he'll take Indigo back to the ranch to heal. You keep the money you win. You'll have enough to keep you going when we divorce. I'll even do something stupid so it's all on me. You can walk away free and clear with your head high."

"Why, Chase? I still don't get it. Why not just tell your father to go…" She stopped before using the word on the tip of her tongue and corrected it to "Uh…take a flying leap? You're an adult. Why let him control you?"

She had a point, but his reasons were so messed up, a battery of psychiatrists would have a field day trying to figure out his family dynamics. "Look up the term *dysfunctional family* in the dictionary. The definition will be two words. *The Barrons*." He lifted one shoulder in a negligent shrug. "But you deserve the truth. I'm weak, Savannah. And a coward, pretty much. My father is a right bastard, and he's ridden roughshod over every one of us. He's threatened to fire me. Chance fixed the family trust so I'll be taken care of, but I wouldn't be in charge of Barron Entertainment."

He pushed off the table and strode to the windows. Las Vegas and the desert beyond spread before him in a seemingly endless vista. "I *like* what I do. Hell, I love it. But more important, I'm good at it. I wasn't good at anything growing up."

Chase snapped his mouth shut and stiffened. What the hell was wrong with him? He never revealed his true thoughts to anyone. Not even Cash, especially not now. He wasn't smart like Chance. He wasn't a leader like Clay. He wasn't honorable like Cord. And he sure wasn't like his twin, always putting the family before his own needs. Quite the opposite, in fact.

"We're not consummating the marriage."

Thankfully, her words interrupted his reverie. He turned his head, and heat curled deep inside as he swept his gaze over her. She really was beautiful in a down-to-earth way. He didn't miss the widening of her eyes, the quick intake of breath that swelled her breasts or the delicate shiver that skittered over her skin as he watched her.

"But we are sleeping in the same bed," he countered.

"Whoa. What?"

"We have to convince my father we're married. That means you sleep in my bed—with me—while he's here. You'll be headed out on the circuit after the rodeo, right?"

She nodded, apprehension warring with something else in her expression. Was that interest? Maybe a touch of curious lust? He liked that idea.

"We won't necessarily be together under one roof. Except when you come back here and there's a long stretch between your appearances."

"Why can't I go home to Oklahoma?"

"Because you'll be my wife, and since this is my

main residence, you'll come here. I'll arrange for permanent stable and training facilities for you." He walked back across the room and stopped in front of her so she had to crane her neck to look at him.

"We work together in public to make sure no one gets the wrong perception." He resisted the urge to cup her cheek. "We'll paint a picture of a happy couple in love. I'll have Tucker set up accounts for you at the hotel's boutiques. Buy whatever you need. I promise not to drag you to a fancy party unless absolutely necessary, and I'll prep you before that happens. We'll hold hands in public. Smile at each other. Do that sort of thing. Here in the apartment, when we're alone, we act as normal. My bed is huge. You can put pillows down the middle or whatever you need to feel comfortable. I promise not to put the moves on you."

He held out his hand. "Do we have a deal?"

Savvie's palm itched, and the muscles in her right arm contracted in preparation for the shake that would seal her fate—at least for the next year. A look crossed Chase's face as his gaze swept over her, much as it had when he stood across the room. This time, the impact was immediate. She couldn't ignore the thrill zinging through her. She couldn't help it. Despite being a royal jerk, he was sexy. And handsome. And charming. And she was a red-blooded Oklahoma cowgirl who knew prime breeding stock when she saw it. The guy had good genes—and jeans, or at least slacks. She shook her head to clear the sexual tension building in her middle. Getting involved with him was Trouble with a capital *T*.

But could she afford to walk away? He was offering

her the chance to fulfill her dream. Making this deal with the devil would ensure she could keep Indy, and he'd get the treatment he needed. She wouldn't have to tuck tail and sneak home. All she had to do was live in a fishbowl for the next twelve months. She shouldn't trust this guy any farther than she could throw him but some twisted part of her urged her to accept him at face value. He was a scandal waiting to happen, but his boyish charm held a touch of uncertainty with a side helping of wistful desperation.

"Deal." She raised her hand and he clasped it. Had she been a romantic, she would have expected a bolt of energy or awareness or some mystical connection to surge between them at the touch of their hands. But she felt nothing beyond smooth skin, gentle pressure and a sense of relief.

"Excellent. We have a lot to do between now and Friday." He whipped out his phone and pressed a number. "Tucker, I need you in the apartment." He hung up and hit a second number. He listened for a moment, then left a message. "Chance, draw up the paperwork we discussed. Courier the originals out here. I'll have Tucker witness and notarize. Thanks, bro."

He paused to wink at her. "I'll have Security give you a code for the elevator. Tuck will take you downstairs to shop. In the meantime, call Kade. Tell him exactly what you need." He turned away, already keying in the next number on his cell.

"Uh… Chase?"

He refocused his attention her. "Yeah, kitten?"

Huh. She'd gone from *wildcat* to *kitten*. She wasn't quite sure how to process that. Instead, she pushed forward. "I…um… I don't mean to be greedy or anything, but could I talk to Kade about borrowing two horses? If I have a roping horse to go with a barrel horse, I can double up on my events and points. I won't keep them or anything, after…well…next year. I just want Indy. I'll ride the other horses, but they'll still belong to you. Okay?"

His gaze narrowed and then cleared as she babbled. "Babe, whatever you need. Don't worry about expenses. I have money. Feel free to spend it. And those horses are yours. No matter what." With that, he moved away from her and into the recessed space that served as his office, his phone pressed to his ear.

She dug her cell phone out of her pocket and dialed Kade. She didn't expect the first words out of his mouth.

"Are you out of your freaking mind?"

"Uh, hi, Kade. I'm fine, thanks. How are you?"

"Pissed, little girl. You need to get as far away from Las Vegas as you can get."

"Nope. Can't do that."

"What have you done?"

"We shook on it, Kade." She huffed out a breath heavy enough to stir the thick strand of hair straggling over her forehead. "Look, this is a good deal for me. If I don't take it, I slink home so my mother and that jackass warming her bed can rub it in my face. I can't do that. I won't do it. Chase is offering me a deal I can't walk away from."

"You don't know him."

"Yeah, I do. I read the tabloids. I know he's a womanizing jerk face with entitlement issues."

An uncomfortable silence stretched between them

before Kade's voice whispered in her ear. "*Itek soba*, he'll break your heart."

Sister of the horse. Kade hadn't called her that in a long time. Using the childhood Chickasaw nickname he'd given her brought home just how worried he was. "No, he won't. I'd have to love him first, and that is so not gonna happen, *anakfi*." She used the Choctaw word for *brother*. "There's paperwork so we're both covered. I have to do this, Kade. You know that. Are you going to help me?"

"Of course I am, Savvie. But I damn well don't have to like it."

"So... I need two horses."

"I figured you might. I have two Crown B bred horses I think will work. Tansy Reed's been working Cimarron. He's rough and still needs seasoning but he's fast, and I think the two of you will work well. He has a soft mouth."

"Okay." Wow. Tansy Reed was *the* premier barrel racer and trainer. She'd retired from the rodeo circuit to raise her family and train horses. "What about a roping horse?"

"Have the perfect guy for you. I've been working Big Red myself. He's quick, responsive and I swear he knows where the calf is gonna be before I do. I've also done both heading and heeling with him in case you want to add team roping."

"I'll keep it in mind. Don't have a partner for that." She pursed her lips, considering. "Yet. I'll look around, see who's available."

"I'll load up and head that way today. I'll be there by Thursday morning. You'll have time to ride them both, and they'll have their ground legs back before the rodeo starts."

A knock on the door caught her attention. "Call me when you get here. I'll meet you at Clark County. Somebody's at the door. I gotta go, Kade."

His heavy sigh hung between them. "Are you sure, little girl?"

"Yeah. Everything is gonna be fine. You'll take care of Indy for me, right?"

"You don't even have to ask."

She ended the call, and when she caught Chase's attention, he waved her toward the door. She opened it, only to be confronted by a handsome man. He vaguely resembled Chase, except instead of sharp brown eyes, this man's were a startling blue and his hair was a dark russet brown instead of black.

"Huh." He stared at her, obviously not very impressed. "I can't wait until Uncle Cyrus gets a load of you. Let's go."

"Go?"

"Yeah. I'm Tucker, soon to be your cousin-in-law. I'm taking you shopping. Clothes. Truck. Trailer. Sound familiar?"

"Before we sign the paperwork?"

"Nothing goes into your name until after the marriage."

"Oh." Savannah wasn't quite sure how she felt about that.

Tucker looked over the top of her head and called to Chase. "We'll stop by Security and get her into the system. See you for dinner."

He grabbed her arm and tugged, but she jerked free. "Wait. My purse."

Reaching around her, Tucker pulled the door closed. "You won't need it."

Five

Chase watched Tucker tease Savannah, surprised at the burn in his chest. His cousin and the woman he planned to marry had spent the previous afternoon picking out a pickup, a fancy horse trailer, getting her added to his credit accounts with a checking account of her own and into the hotel's security system so she could access his apartment. He'd spent the day auditioning some new showgirls, dealing with a situation on the casino floor and listening to his big brother rant about how stupid Chase was being. That was easy for Chance to say. He'd found and married the girl of his dreams. True, Dad had done his best to break them up, but Chance told the old man off and went merrily on his way. Chance didn't have the old man breathing down his neck, complete with a forced marriage looming.

If he had to take the plunge, Chase was darn sure he'd be doing it on his terms, not his dad's. He studied the woman he'd be marrying within the next twenty-four hours. This morning, he had a conference call with investors and the architect of the new hotel project in the Bahamas. He'd need to rent a car for Savannah to drive until the new pickup and trailer were ready. Kade was due to arrive in the morning, and she'd be out at the fairgrounds all day with the ranch foreman and the new horses.

He planned a fast trip to the Clark County Marriage License Bureau, an office open 24/7 due to Vegas's reputation for quickie weddings, for later in the afternoon. They'd get married Thursday night so it was a done deal before the old man hit Vegas on Friday.

"Hope you don't mind."

Chase pulled his head into the conversation and stared at Tucker. "Mind what?"

"That I'm taking Savannah to Leather and Lace."

Savannah choked and coffee spewed out her nose. She grabbed a napkin, coughing, while Chase thumped her on the back. "Can you breathe?" When she nodded, he still watched her to be sure, but answered Tucker. "I don't have a problem with that. See about getting her some custom boots. They won't have them ready before she heads out, but we'll have them here the first time she comes home."

"Uh, hello. Right here. I don't need boots. Or anything else…leather."

Both men glanced at her and Tucker chuckled. "L and L is the premier Western store in the area. The few things you found in the boutique downstairs won't go far."

Chase nodded. "We need to fill up your half of my closet. And Tuck's right. You need new clothes."

Her face turned red again, and she pushed out of her chair, all but spitting mad. "What's wrong with my clothes?"

It was totally perverse of him to enjoy her anger but dang if it wasn't fun. "Darlin', those jeans are nothing but holes held together with a prayer. You need new work boots. You need new boots for the arena and—" he propped one booted foot up on the table "—I know how comfortable custom boots are. As my wife, you need to upgrade. It's expected."

She sputtered and spit and shoved his foot off. "You musta been raised in a barn, boy. Don't you know better'n to put your feet on a table with food?"

He grinned and was almost sorry she'd be taking off soon. He'd like the chance to get to know her better and do a whole lot more teasing. He liked her curves, and the way her expressions revealed her thoughts. Maybe he would do a little seducing along the way. Before he could think too deeply on that urge, Tucker's phone pinged.

"Courier from Chance is here." Tuck left to meet the person Security was escorting up.

Chase leaned back in his chair and studied Savannah. He hadn't missed her quick inhalation or the widening of her eyes at the mention of the arrival of the prenuptial paperwork. "Second thoughts, kitten?"

Her eyes wouldn't quite meet his when she replied. "No. Yes. A little." She squared her shoulders and met his gaze. "What about you? You can walk away and not be stuck with me."

"Something tells me I'm getting the better deal."

He realized he'd said that out loud when he saw the surprised look on Savannah's face. But before he could add anything, a very feminine squeal filled the air, and a bundle of feminine curves landed in his lap.

"Chase! I'm so glad Chance sent me. I've been wanting to see you for…like…forever." The girl in his lap cupped his cheeks and plastered kisses all over his face. He would kill his brother the next time he saw Chance. "I've never been to Vegas. I took some comp time so I can stay a couple of days, and you can show me around and we can—"

He cut off her babbling by clamping his hands around her waist and lifting her out of his lap. A glance at Savannah made him wince. She tried to hide her feelings, but she wasn't quick enough. He saw anger, and was that a little hurt, too? She definitely wasn't happy, and he couldn't blame her.

"Where's the paperwork from Chance, Debbie?"

"Darla. My name is Darla." The girl huffed in displeasure, one hand on her hip, the other holding a manila envelope.

"Oh, yeah. Right. Whatever."

Tucker relieved Darla of the sealed envelope. Using a pocket knife, he slit it open while Darla glowered. After a few moments, her eyes flicked to Savannah.

"Who're you?"

"This is my fiancée," Chase answered before Savannah could.

Savvie wasn't very happy when Darla bent over from the waist, laughing hard. She started to tamp down the remark on the tip of her tongue and then gave up on being circumspect. That wasn't really her style. Reaching over to take Chase's hand, she put her best snooty face on. "Chase, darlin', you really need to stop screwin' the hired help. They get so pushy and all uppity when you do."

Tucker lost it. He laughed so hard tears squeezed out from the corners of his eyes. Chase stared at her, biting his lips, but his eyes danced with amusement.

"Oh, my God. You can't be serious, Chase. She's… she's…"

Chase flicked his gaze to the girl, and Savannah was really glad he wasn't looking at her with that expression on his face. "She's the woman I'm marrying, Darla. You'd be wise to remember that. I'll call Chance about sending the papers back. For now, I suggest you head to the airport and catch the first flight back to Oklahoma City."

"But…but… I flew out here in the company jet."

"The company jet is reserved for family and employees. Effective as of right now, you are neither."

Savannah couldn't prevent her jaw from dropping. She squeezed Chase's hand and started to say something, but Chase shushed her with a look. She clamped her mouth shut and waited.

"I'll show you out, Darla." Tucker took the girl's arm and tugged her toward the door. A few minutes later, he returned and shut the door. "Security has her. They'll escort her to the airport, and make sure she's on a plane. I'll call Chance, fill him in."

"Hey." Savannah quietly asked for Chase's attention. "You didn't need to fire her."

"Yeah, I did. You're going to be my wife, Savannah. Legally and binding. No one talks to you that way. No one makes that kind of assumption."

She studied his expression. He was serious and

being truthful. Wow. Who knew the guy had some depth, and maybe a modicum of honor, after all? "Okay. But just so you know, I'm pretty good at taking care of myself."

Chase and Tucker exchanged looks, then both burst out laughing. "Hired help," Tucker sputtered.

"Pushy and uppity." Chase snorted, and laughed harder.

Savannah crossed her arms over her chest. "Dang. It wasn't even that snarky."

"Finish your breakfast, wildcat. Tucker wants to go all metrosexual and pick out a wardrobe for you. Let him."

"Okay." Savannah chewed on her bottom lip a moment.

"What?"

"What what?"

Chase's gaze lasered in on her mouth. "You look like you want to ask something. What is it?"

"Oh. Just…uh…wondering what you'll be doing today while I go spend gobs of your money?"

"Running my empire." He leaned in to whisper in her ear. "And I doubt you'd spend my money at all if I weren't forcing it on you. Just be back by four this afternoon. We need to get the marriage license."

Her breath caught, and her body went a little haywire, not that she would let her reaction show—especially since they had an audience. She'd be smart to remember that Chase Barron was a rascal—a very sexy one who used women without a shred of guilt. Pushing back from the table, she retreated. The expression on his face told her he knew what she was doing. She didn't really care. She needed space.

"Before you go, we both need to sign the prenup."

"Oh, right."

Tuck watched her go through the racks. He was flirting with the salesclerk, but he also made note of what Savannah was doing. Every time she checked the price tag of an item, he snagged it and told the clerk to hang in it the dressing room.

"Stop doing that, Savannah. If you like something, try it on. If you want it, it's yours."

"Yeah, easy for you to say."

The negligent lift of one shoulder indicated he didn't care about her feelings on the matter. "Look, hon, my cousin very often leaps without considering the consequences. I read the prenup. I know what you're getting out of this deal. I've also spent time with you. You aren't comfortable with this. I don't know what your reasons are but they have nothing to do with Chase's money."

It was her turn to offer a desultory shrug. "People are still gonna talk."

"Yes, they will. You need to be prepared for that. Especially since Chase won't always be around to shield you."

"What does that mean?" she faced Tucker and asked. "Shield me from who?"

"His family. The media. Anyone familiar with the Barron name."

Chase would deal with his family so that wasn't a concern. The media? Yeah, that would suck. "Maybe I can fly under the radar. I won't use his name when I enter my events."

"Sorry, babe. That won't work. The Barron name

will be plastered all over your truck and trailer. And Chase isn't exactly shy and retiring."

That got an eye roll. "No kidding." She closed her eyes and tilted her head back in an attempt to ease the tight muscles in her neck. After taking a deep breath, she opened her eyes and offered Tucker her I'm-gonna-do-this face. Then she spoiled it all by asking, "He's not going to be monogamous, is he?"

Tucker's expression was full of sympathy. "I doubt it. But you'll have to be."

She laughed at that. "I haven't had a date in two years." Heading to the dressing room, she left Tucker standing there with his mouth hanging open.

Four hours later, they walked out of Leather and Lace with bags and boxes and more clothes and pairs of boots than Savannah had owned in her entire life. Tucker had convinced her to change from her jeans and T into a dress that reminded her a little of traditional Choctaw garb. Embroidery, ribbons, a full skirt, all in natural colors that Tucker insisted set off her golden-brown skin and dark hair. And new boots. Expensive new boots that fit her feet like gloves. The boot maker in L and L had spent an hour measuring, drawing and discussing leathers, heels, colors and stitching designs. Tucker refused to let her see the bill but she'd seen the price tags. Who in their right mind dropped almost twenty thousand dollars on clothes? Oh, yeah. Chase Barron and the women he was used to dating, for sure, but not plain ol' Savannah Wolfe.

The last person she expected to see was Chase leaning up against Tucker's sleek Mercedes SUV, looking all fashion-model perfect in his tailored suit, starched shirt and designer tie. The slow grin lighting up his face did all sorts of things to her bits and pieces—which she needed to ignore because she was not letting Chase get under her skirts. Skin. She meant skin. And he was just slick enough that he could charm his way right there if she gave him any room at all.

"You buy the store out?"

Blushing, she tried to say something but only stammered out nonsense.

Chase was suddenly there, his hands gently gripping her waist. "Whoa, kitten. Breathe. I was joking."

Taking his advice, she inhaled several times. "I'm not a gold digger." She murmured it under her last deep breath, but he heard her.

"I know that, Savannah."

She stared into his eyes. "Do you? Do you really?"

Studying her face, Chase realized she was truly worried. "Yeah, kitten, I do." He dropped his head to place a kiss on her forehead. "You aren't Debbie."

"Darla."

"What? Oh, yeah, right. Darla. You aren't her, Savannah. You aren't that producer's wife. You aren't those two backup singers in Nashville. You're just… you. You're in a tight spot, and so am I. My money will help you out of yours. You marrying me gets my dad off my back. Trust me, I'd spend a small fortune to ensure that."

"You are definitely doing that—spending a fortune." She cocked her head to one side and studied him. He met her gaze without blinking. "Why me, Chase?"

"You've asked that before."

"I still don't get it. Why me?"

"Because you *are* you. You don't want my money.

My wealth makes you uncomfortable. You're honest. In my world, that makes you pretty much one of a kind."

"Wow. I don't think I want to live in your world, if that's the case." She didn't smile at him and he could feel her sincerity.

"Not always a good place to be, but I have the feeling it's gonna be a little easier with you in it."

Tucker cleared his throat with a discreet cough. "Cuz, take your lady to a late lunch. I'll head back to the hotel with her stuff and see that it's put away in your apartment." He off-loaded everything into his SUV and disappeared, leaving the two of them standing in the parking lot.

"What are you hungry for?" Chase's libido almost took him to his knees as Savannah stared up at him and licked her lips.

"Hungry for?"

He knew what he was hungry for. Keeping his hands-off promise might just kill him. He still couldn't pinpoint what drew him to this untamed cowgirl but something damn sure did. "Food, kitten."

"What are *you* hungry for?"

Her. He wanted to taste her—her mouth and other places. He willed his body to behave and plastered an easy smile on his face. Poker. They were playing emotional poker and he was a high-stakes player in this game. He made a quick decision and offered her a choice.

"Mexican or Chinese?"

"Mexican."

Hot and spicy. Just like her. He all but groaned at the direction his thoughts kept taking and gestured toward his Jag to cover his reaction to her.

Chase shared his favorite hole-in-the-wall taque-ria with her. He didn't bring people here, except for Tucker, but his cousin didn't count as *people*. He'd never even brought his brothers here. It felt right to be sitting at the scarred wooden table with Savannah, sharing street tacos and listening to her talk about life on the rodeo circuit. Their conversation fell into an easy rhythm, and he found himself sharing anecdotes of his childhood and the scrapes he and his twin got into.

More at ease with her and his decision, Chase paid the bill, and they headed to the marriage license bureau. They shuffled through the line, with more than a few covert glances cast their direction. He'd hoped to keep things low-key but cell phones were not-so-surreptitiously pointed at them. Savannah appeared unruffled, and his admiration ratcheted up another notch. That was good. She'd need to be unflappable when word of their marriage leaked, and they faced his father. Cyrus didn't lose gracefully, and he'd do his damnedest to make them all pay.

Six

With license in hand, Chase steered the Jag toward the hotel. They hadn't driven even a block before his cell phone rang. He punched the Bluetooth button, but Tucker didn't give him a chance to speak.

"Mayday, Chase."

He exchanged a humorous glance with Savannah as he answered. "Can't be that bad, bud. What's up?"

"Wanna bet? Oh, wait. This is Vegas. I don't know if we have a spy or what, but your old man is on his way. Early."

Chase growled. "Debbie."

"Darla," Savannah corrected.

Watching the traffic ahead, Chase made a quick decision. "We'll get married now. I'm pulling into the Candelabra Wedding Chapel as we speak. When is the old man due to arrive?"

"My own spy says late tonight. After midnight."

"Okay. We'll stay out late."

"I'll cover."

"You always do, cuz. Thanks."

"Don't thank me. I'm keeping track, Chase. You owe me big-time." Tucker chuckled, then dead air hummed over the car's speakers.

Chase parked and cut the engine and swiveled to face Savannah. "Well, kitten, this is it. Your last chance to back out."

He didn't hold his breath, despite the inclination to do so. He was all sorts of a jerk for doing this, but standing up to his father without this pretense of a marriage wasn't something he felt capable of managing. Besides, Savannah needed help. It wasn't like she didn't benefit from this deal.

Her chest swelled as she breathed deeply. Her hands remained in her lap, clasped, and far more white-knuckled that he cared to see. Maybe she would cut and run. He wouldn't blame her if she did. Dealing with him, even on a limited basis, wouldn't be easy. He continued to watch her, waiting for her answer.

Savannah curled her lips between her teeth, straightened her shoulders and faced him. "Let's do this."

Whew! He'd dodged a bullet, and he knew it. Liking the woman he'd be tied to for a year even more, he winked and opened his door. "Yes, ma'am. Let's git 'er done."

They walked into what was essentially a lavender boudoir. Satin draped the walls, and there were plush velvet sofas and a dark purple runner that led them straight to a woman with swirls of silver curls—curls faintly tinged with purple. She greeted them with a fire-engine red smile. Her lace cocktail gown was the exact same tint as the walls.

"Welcome to the Candelabra Wedding Chapel!" Her eyes landed on the paper in Chase's hand. "Oh, excellent. You already have your license. So many young lovers don't, you know. Come, come." The woman clapped her hands in glee as she led them toward a long counter and an old-fashioned brass cash register. She slipped behind the counter and pushed a gold menu toward them. "We have many packages available and will happily create a custom experience for a slight extra charge."

Glancing at the list of services, Chase pointed to the bottom—and most expensive—package. "That one. How soon?"

"No waiting, dearie. That is our Stardust ceremony. Very romantic." The woman turned shrewd eyes on Savannah. "Do you need a wedding gown, lovey? We have a wide selection to choose from. Only a little added charge to rent."

Chase glanced over at Savannah. She looked fine to him. Her outfit—an airy skirt, beribboned blouse and a fringed shawl—would be considered Western chic. It'd do. "What she's wearing is suitable."

A flash of disappointment registered on the woman's face before her mask fell back into place. "Flowers? Rings?"

Oh, yeah. He studied the menu more closely. The package he'd picked came with a set of his and her gold wedding bands and a silk flower bouquet. That'd be enough. "We'll take the ones that come with the Stardust."

"Fine." The hostess sounded a bit snippy but she

pulled out a velvet ring tray. "Pick any two on the bottom three rows."

He selected a band and held it out to Savannah to try on. Too small. He grabbed the next ring in the row. It was slightly too large, but again, it would suffice. Under the hawk-eyed gaze of the woman, he picked one for himself. He didn't wear jewelry so it would end up in his drawer later.

Moments later, the woman handed a bundle of white silk roses wrapped with satin ribbon to Savannah. "Do you have a witness?"

The front door opened with an electronic rendition of the opening notes of "Moonlight Serenade" and Tucker walked in.

"Yes," Chase told the woman. "We do."

"Will this be cash or credit card?"

Tucker reached into his pocket and pulled out a thick fold of bills. "Cash. How much?"

The woman punched the keys on the old cash register, muttering to herself. "That will be three hundred twenty-four dollars and twenty-nine cents, including tax."

She sorted the cash into the register drawer, then ushered them through a doorway. The room wasn't huge and carried on the purple theme. The hostess—called "Mother" by the officiant, a man with a lavender pompadour—seated herself at a linen-draped table and punched the button on a karaoke machine. She picked up a cheap digital camera and began taking pictures. A photo package was part of the deal.

Tucker offered to walk Savannah down the aisle—all six feet of it. She had never been a girlie-girl dreaming of her Prince Charming and a fairy-tale wedding, but this was pretty much a joke. Tucker's expression was studied, though he offered her hand a sympathetic pat where it rested just below the crook of his elbow. Means to an end, she reminded herself. That's all this was. Chase Barron wasn't a knight in shining armor, and while she might appear to be in distress—financially, anyway—she was no shy and retiring damsel in need of rescue. She'd rescue herself, thank you very much. Raising her chin, she squared her shoulders and focused on the man waiting about eight steps away.

The minister, dressed in a gray tux trimmed in violet and wearing a lilac-dyed fur cape, stood between two tall brass candelabras with electric candles flickering in time to the music. A medley of Liberace's music filtered over the minister's words. Loving and obeying were mentioned, richer, poorer, in sickness and health, and that whole death disclaimer. Twelve months. Fifty-two weeks. Three hundred and sixty-five days. If Savannah had a calculator, she'd figure the hours and minutes until she could return to Vegas and file for divorce.

"I do," she said when prompted.

"I do." When his turn came, Chase sounded about as enthusiastic as she did. He slid the too-big ring on her finger, and she made a mental note to get some tape to make it fit.

"You may now kiss the bride."

Her breath froze in her chest, and she couldn't even swallow. She'd been staring at the knot in Chase's tie during the recitation of their vows, but now she had to look up. Her gaze met his, and his heated expression thawed her paralysis. Before she could inhale, his mouth lowered to hers, capturing her lips. He nibbled on them, nipping her bottom lip before sweeping his tongue over it to ease the slight sting from his bite. One arm curved around her waist, pulling her hips tight against his. He was definitely happy to see her.

Her blood drained from her brain to parts more feminine as his free hand cupped her cheek and tilted her head so he could deepen the kiss. She locked her knees to keep them from shaking, and her eyelids fluttered to a close. Her nipples pebbled as her breasts encountered his chest, and she gripped his lapels in sheer self-defense.

Savannah had no clue how much time had elapsed before she surfaced from the sexual haze of that kiss. She blinked open her eyes, caught the smug satisfaction in Chase's expression and hated that she'd fallen for his ploy. The man was a player, plain and simple. And she'd entered into a marriage of convenience with him. Any feelings she might have purely complicated matters.

A discreet cough caused her to loosen her hands, give a push against Chase's muscled chest and step away. Tucker looked amused, and Mother and the faux Liberace appeared ready to proceed with pictures. Chase just preened. Savvie managed not to slap the smirk off his face.

They posed for pictures, her expression as fake as their marriage. In name only, she reminded herself. But what a name. Ten minutes later, she walked out with a CD of photos documenting essentially a marriage for hire, a gold-plated wedding band that didn't fit her finger and a bedraggled bouquet of fake flowers. That pretty much summed up everything about her. They should do a reality show about her: *My Big Fat Fake Wedding*.

In the parking lot, Tucker dropped a kiss on the top of her head and softly squeezed her shoulders. "I'll head back and cut Cyrus off at the pass when he arrives. I'd tell you to check into a suite at one of the other hotels, but that would be bad for business—the CEO of Barron Entertainment spending his wedding night somewhere other than his own resort? Yeah, no. I did, however, make reservations for a private dining room, lakeside, at Solstice. They've agreed to stay open—for a rather large fee—until the two of you leave."

Savvie shifted her gaze between the two men. "Solstice?"

"Five-star restaurant. Great steaks. And froufrou food," Chase explained. "The main thing is we'll have privacy and good food until Tuck calls to say the coast is clear."

Dinner was definitely a five-star affair. The room was lavish—like something from a Hollywood blockbuster. They'd been whisked through the line by the manager himself and escorted through the magnificently decorated restaurant to their "room." The place reminded her of a romance-book cover—something with sheikhs or barbarian princes. The man sitting across from her was certainly rich enough to be a prince, and handsome enough to grace the cover of a romance. She studied him over the rim of her champagne flute. She'd lost track of how many glasses Chase plied her with, but she admitted she liked the floaty feeling.

Chase retrieved her glass and set it on the table before taking her hand and urging her to stand. "Let's dance."

"Um…" She did her best not to stumble. "I'm not much of a dancer." Savvie could Texas two-step and do the Cotton Eyed Joe. Barely. But fancy dancing? Like waltzes or fox-trots or something?

"There's not much to it, kitten. We put our arms around each other and sway in time to the music."

"Oh. Okay. I can do that." She could, right?

He led her to the small dance floor, and a song that was vaguely familiar teased their feet to move. True to his word, he curled his arms around her waist and she put hers around his neck.

She was about five-eight in her boots and he stood almost a head taller. Her cheek nestled comfortably against the hollow of his shoulder and with her ear pressed against his chest, she could hear his heartbeat keeping time with the music.

Her fingers played with the fringe of black hair covering his collar. His hair was thick and soft, a little too long, but she liked the feel of it against her skin.

He was definitely handsome. Square jaw that was sculpted but not knife sharp. Straight nose, high cheekbones. Eyes the color of hot coffee. She stared into those eyes for a long moment, her hands dropping to his broad, muscular shoulders. She read humor there. Mischief. A hint of lust and…a secret. Chase Barron had secrets. He blinked and the moment passed.

Tall, dark, handsome—and rich to boot. The Barrons were Oklahoma royalty. A local paper once ran a cartoon depicting Cyrus Barron seated on a throne, wearing a cowboy hat with a tiara, like the ones rodeo queens wore. His five sons stood behind him, each a prince carrying the symbol of his specialty—government, law, oil, entertainment and security. A king wearing a "Midas" name tag along with caricatures of various world leaders lined up looking for handouts. Mr. Barron bought the paper in retaliation. Now that she'd been exposed to the reality of Barron wealth? Yeah, that cartoon was pretty much dead-on.

Chase Barron had everything going for him. What was not to love? Her brain wanted to go there, figure out all the cons, but it was foggy in her head and he smelled good. The music was relaxing. Expensive champagne buzzed in her blood.

Then he kissed her. The world pretty much stopped. Her feet stopped moving as her hands tangled in his hair. She pressed against him, her hips seeking the welcoming hardness of his body. His tongue teased her mouth open, swept inside, seduced her with a slow, sensual mating.

His phone buzzed. Chase didn't break the kiss but she felt him pull out his cell. He whispered into the kiss, "All clear, kitten. Time to go home."

Savvie shot straight up in bed, heart pounding and ears aching from a high-pitched screech. She couldn't remember where she was, or what had happened last night. Drunk. Chase had gotten her drunk on champagne. She'd fallen asleep—okay, passed out—in his car. She didn't remember him carrying her to his apartment, barely remembered undressing in the bathroom, then falling into bed. She panicked, but calmed when she realized she wore a tank and sleep pants. That was good. The rest was bad. Her mouth felt like it was stuffed with cotton, and her brain hurt. A lot. The screaming didn't help. She squinted her eyes closed, opened them, stared.

A blonde woman in a designer dress that probably cost more than Savvie's entire wardrobe—well, her wardrobe before yesterday, anyway—and wearing shoes looking like they'd hurt to walk in stood in the doorway of the bedroom. The screams continued as the woman's face turned red, and she jabbed her index finger in Savvie's direction.

"What are you doing in my fiancé's bed? Getoutgetoutgetout! How dare you!"

What the hell? Savvie's brain caught up with her hearing. Fiancé? Chase didn't mention having a fiancée when he'd proposed this crazy arrangement. He'd mentioned a woman his father wanted him to marry, but he'd said there was nothing finalized. Before she could say anything, the woman screeched again, and two men appeared—one tall, one shorter and rounder.

"Who are you?" the tall one demanded.

Savannah had to think a minute. This was obviously Cyrus Barron, Chase's father. The man had the same look—dark hair but with silver at the temples, piercing brown eyes the color of frozen coffee, high cheekbones and a sharp chin that was currently jutting in her direction. She threw back the covers and climbed out of bed. Better to face them standing on two feet. Luckily, she wasn't one for sexy lingerie. Her spaghetti-strap camisole and cotton sleep pants hid her assets from the appraising looks she received from the men.

"Yes, just who are you?" the woman repeated.

It was on the tip of her tongue to retort, "Savannah

Wolfe," but she wasn't. Not anymore. For at least the next twelve months, she was Savannah Barron. So that's how she answered the question.

Seven

"Barron?" The three all spoke at once.

"Yes. Barron. Technically, I suppose I'm Mrs. Chase Barron." Where the hell was her so-called husband? If Chase had cut and run to leave her facing this alone she'd turn him into a steer just as soon as she got her hands on a knife.

"That's impossible." The woman looked both shocked and hurt, and her voice trembled.

"According to our marriage certificate, it's not only possible but true."

"But Chase is mine." The blonde turned to the slightly rotund man at her side and stamped her foot. "Daddy, you promised him to me."

Seriously? Savannah couldn't choke back the laughter bubbling in her throat. "Sorry to disappoint you, princess, but *I'm* married to Chase."

"But you can't be. Daddy, make her go away. Chase is mine. Write her a check or something."

Ouch. That hit a little too close to home, but while she didn't love Chase, Savvie couldn't really wish this bimbo on him. "Write me a check?" Her voice came out soft but clipped and coated in icicles.

"You just need to go away."

"Since I'm his wife that's not happenin'."

"No, you aren't. You can't be his wife."

"Want to see the license?" She hoped it had been legally filed. Maybe that's where Chase had gone. If so, she wouldn't fix him. Yet.

"It's a fake. It has to be. You trapped him into this. Do you have him tied up and drugged?"

Savvie stood there with her mouth hanging open. "Seriously? You think I drugged Chase Barron, dragged him off to marry me and even now have him tied up somewhere?" She gestured toward the bed behind them. "Are you stupid or something?"

"You can't talk to me that way."

"Sure I can."

Luckily, Chase picked that moment to slide into the room. She hadn't heard him come into the apartment.

He skirted his father, the other man and the woman, coming straight to Savvie's side. Chase curled his arm around her shoulder and dropped a kiss on her temple. "Morning, wildcat. Sorry I wasn't here when you woke up. Security called. We had a situation on the casino floor I had to take care of."

"No worries, hoss. I was just getting to know—" she waved her hand at the three other people "—them. We were discussing the status of our marriage."

"Yeah, I gathered that. You want to throw on some clothes? I'll order up breakfast."

"Works for me."

Chase turned her in his arms and dropped a kiss on her surprised mouth. His eyes twinkled as he winked at her. "Love ya, kitten," he murmured. Then he was gone, ushering their guests out of the bedroom by herding them in front of him and shutting the door.

She stood there, missing the warmth of his body and wondering what had just happened. His words were a throwaway, meant for their audience, but they still singed a spot next to her heart. Savvie had to be very careful from here on out. This man was proving to be most unexpected—in all the wrong ways.

Out in the living room, Chase dialed room service and ordered up a breakfast buffet. He was very careful to keep Janiece on the opposite side of any piece of furniture he could use to obstruct her from approaching him. Hopefully, Savannah wouldn't take long to appear. He hadn't meant for her to face down the old man alone. Chase would still have been in bed with her when his father arrived if the morning-shift pit boss hadn't alerted Security, who then alerted him and Tucker, about a card cheat on the floor. The guy had already taken the casino for half a million before they could verify he was cheating and then deal with the situation.

After their late-night arrival, Chase had figured his father and the Carrolls would sleep in. He'd figured wrong. Then it occurred to him that they'd accessed his apartment on their own. From the looks of things, Savannah had not gotten out of bed to answer the door.

Tucker had been with him down in the casino. That meant his father had access to Chase's personal space. Whoever had given Cyrus the ability to get in was fired. Period. No second chances. Chase hired people who were loyal to him. Not to his father.

The door to the bedroom popped open and Savvie strolled out. Chase immediately forgot about the security problems. Dang, but the woman looked fine. She wore a new pair of jeans that sculpted her long, muscular legs and her very nice butt. The lacy T-shirt left just enough to his imagination, and he shifted uncomfortably, a move his father noted. Chase plastered on his happy groom face—which was far less difficult than it should be given the circumstances—and held his hand out for her to join him. He attempted to read her expression. This was the first huge test of their fabricated relationship, since getting his father to believe their marriage was real hinged on her actions.

Savannah approached with a smile and took his hand without hesitation. She sidled up to him, slipping under his arm like doing so was the most natural thing in the world. Chase let out a mental *whew*.

"Are you going to make introductions, hoss?" Her husky voice washed over him, and he had to resist kissing her again.

"Savannah, I'd like you to meet my father, Cyrus Barron, his business associate, Malcolm Carroll, and Mal's daughter, Janiece." Savvie acknowledged each with a dip of her head, but she stayed glued to his side and didn't speak. "Shall we get comfortable while we wait for breakfast?"

"Y'all pardon me a sec while I put some coffee on. My brain doesn't work until I've had that morning shot of caffeine." Savannah disengaged and ducked into the kitchen.

"Dad, Mal, Janiece, make yourselves comfortable. I'll give Savannah a hand." He followed her into the kitchen. The idea of being alone in uncomfortable silence with those three was totally unappealing. The thought of a few stolen moments with Savannah? Priceless.

He watched her set up the coffeemaker, then bustle around the kitchen, getting mugs, sugar and cream, and arranging a serving tray while the coffee dripped into the carafe. She paused to look at him. "What's the plan, Chase?" Her voice was a whisper.

"I meant to be here. Sorry." He'd wanted to kiss her awake but he couldn't admit that to her, especially with her hands-off policy in full force and effect. Still, he hadn't meant for her to face the old man on her own.

She lifted her shoulders in a forgiving shrug. "No biggie. Just FYI? That woman has the voice of a harpy and she was not happy to find me in your bed. Not the way I pictured waking up."

He stepped closer and pulled her into a hug. He couldn't help himself. Easier to plot, he figured, with her ear right there for him to whisper into. "*Our* bed, kitten," he corrected. "Sorry about the hangover. I ordered a bottle of champagne with the orange juice."

"Hair of the dog? No, thanks! I don't normally drink. Besides, that woman pretty much screeched the hangover out of me."

Chase choked back a laugh, then stiffened as his father came through the door and interrupted. "Really, Chase? You can't keep your hands off…*her* with your fiancée in the next room?"

"*Her* name is Savannah, Dad, and she's my wife. Unless you plan on me being a bigamist, I don't have a fiancée."

"Yo. Hello. Standing right here." Savvie pushed away, but didn't leave his side. "I know you're Chase's father, sir. For that you're due respect, but respect goes both ways. Don't talk down to me, and don't treat me like a bimbo. I assure you, I am not one."

Chase winced and wished she'd remained silent. Before he could get between her and his father, Cyrus cut him off.

"I believe you to be a calculating tramp who got her claws into my very impressionable son." The old man pulled a checkbook out of his suit pocket and flipped it open, pen in hand. "Your kind is always after the money. How much to get rid of you?"

Chase made a futile grab for Savvie's arm, but she was out of his reach and right up in his father's face before he could fully react.

"*My* kind? You mean female? Or Choctaw?"

"I will not stand here and allow Chase to make a fool of himself."

"The only person making a fool of himself is you. You walk into our home and make insinuations you have no right to make." She glanced at the checkbook and smiled. "You don't have enough zeros to buy me off, Mr. Barron. I'm married to your son and I intend to stay that way." She turned around and walked back to Chase.

Once again at his side, she confronted his father. "Just FYI? I didn't marry him for his money. If you believe that's the only reason a woman would marry

Chase, then you're a sorry son of a buck and I pity you."

Wow. Chase didn't know whether to cringe, run or kiss her. No one had ever stood up for him like that. He certainly hadn't expected it from a woman he'd just met, whose loyalty he was basically buying. He straightened his shoulders and faced the old man. "We're married, Dad. For better or worse. Get used to the idea." He glanced at the TAG Heuer watch on his wrist. "Breakfast will be here any moment. You and the Carrolls are welcome to stay. Personally, I'd prefer you get the hell out so I can enjoy the small bit of honeymoon we've got left. Just know, if you stay, you will treat my wife with respect."

A loud knock sounded before Cyrus could answer. Chase dropped another kiss on Savvie's temple. "I'll go let room service in, kitten. Can you handle the coffee?"

"Got it, hoss."

He grinned, unable to help himself. "Yeah, you definitely got it, hon."

To say breakfast was strained would have been a huge understatement. Once Tucker arrived, Savvie kept her mouth shut and did her best to ignore Janiece's whining and pitiful attempts at flirting with Chase. He brushed his hand over Savvie's leg every time the other woman opened her mouth, an attempt to let her know things would be okay, she supposed. Cyrus continued to glare, which wasn't conducive to a healthy appetite. Maybe she should have kept her mouth shut. What had possessed her to take on the patriarch of the Barron clan? She needed to stay off Mr. Barron's radar big-time, and antagonizing the man was not the way to make that happen.

She managed to choke down some scrambled eggs and bacon, relying mostly on the strong coffee she'd brewed. Hardly anyone else ate. Just Chase. He shoveled food into his mouth like a bear stocking up for hibernation. Looking at him, one would think everything was hunky-dory. When he pushed his plate away, he reached for the champagne chilling in a bucket of ice, and popped the cork on it. He filled the crystal flutes on the tray next to the ice bucket and passed them around.

Remaining on his feet, he raised his glass in her direction. "Here's to my beautiful wife. She's already made my life better."

He extended his glass toward her, so Savvie carefully clinked hers against his. The fragile crystal pinged. She took a sip, then extended her glass. "And here's to my handsome husband, the man who surprises me constantly."

They clinked again, then touched glasses with the flute Tucker held out. The three of them each took a sip, while the others didn't move, the flutes sitting untouched next to their plates.

"I cannot believe you are participating in this travesty, Tucker." Cyrus turned on his nephew. "I mistakenly believed you were the one with some intelligence and sense."

Savvie's phone picked that moment to ring. She fished it out of her hip pocket, glanced at the screen and cringed inwardly. "I... Sorry. My mother. I need to take this call." She pushed away from the table before either Chase or Tucker could move to hold her chair. She ducked down the hallway as she answered and didn't stop walking until she was in the bedroom with the door shut.

"Mom?"

"You've been holding out on me, Savannah." Her mother's tone grated. Kayla Wolfe had been drinking.

"I don't know what you're talking about."

"Are you pregnant?"

"Excuse me?"

"You heard me. Did that SOB get you pregnant? I saw you and Chase Barron on that *Inside Celebrity* show. They said you got married. At least you were smart enough to get a ring on your finger. Not like some people."

Savannah closed her eyes and resisted the urge to bang her head against the wall. She knew exactly who that "some people" referred to. Every time the Barron name came up, her mother alluded to Kaden's mom, Rose, insinuating she'd had an affair with Cyrus Barron and Kaden was an illegitimate Barron son.

"No, Mom. I'm not pregnant."

"Good. Still, married to a Barron? You better get lots of money to send home to me, baby girl."

A soft rap on the door had her scrambling. "I have to go, Mom."

"Send money, baby. Tom needs a new truck."

Chase opened the door and peeked around its edge, a questioning expression on his face. She waved him in as she signed off. "Bye, Mom."

"Problem?"

She plastered a smile on her face. "No. She was just calling to congratulate us."

"Uh-huh." He brushed two fingers across her cheek.

"Don't lie to me, kitten. And a word to the wise? Don't ever play poker with me. Especially strip poker. I'll have you naked before we finish one hand."

That made her laugh. "Pretty sure that's the truth."

"C'mon, babe. Talk to me."

She gave in to temptation and thunked her forehead against his chest. His arms came around her waist. "Yours isn't the only dysfunctional family in the world." She straightened and tried to smile, but figured it was more of a grimace, judging by Chase's expression. "Don't ever give my mother money. No matter what she says or does."

"Ah."

"Yeah, ah. I'm serious, Chase. She'll whine and wheedle and pull all sorts of crap to get it from you. And warn Tucker, too. Okay?"

"Sure, babe. We'll watch out for her."

"I'm sorry."

"For what?"

"For having a greedy mother. For letting your father get to me."

"Shh." He pulled her back to his chest and held her while he brushed his cheek over the top of her head. "You were pretty darn impressive. Not many people stand up him. Thank you for coming to my defense."

"You're welcome. Now, let's get back so we can make them all go away. We're supposed to be on our honeymoon."

Eight

Chase had hoped their guests would leave while he was in the bedroom with Savannah. Her words were still ricochcting through his brain. Her mother sounded like a piece of work, and he made a mental note to ask Kade about the woman. Savvie's reaction to the phone call left him feeling protective—and concerned. For a moment, he considered throwing money at the problem, then stopped cold. That's what his father would do, was trying to do with Savannah. No, he would follow Savannah's request. No money to her mother. Not without his wife's permission.

He almost tripped. *His wife. Needing—wanting— her permission.* Two totally new concepts for him. He liked the first, oddly enough. Holding her hand as they stepped into the living room, he stopped cold. His father was on the phone, yelling. Janiece looked smug, while her father appeared uncomfortable and was probably wishing he was anywhere but here. Chase seconded the feeling.

"You better fix this, Chance," Cyrus spit into his phone.

That explained the atmosphere. The prenup had been overnighted to Chance and was probably open on his desk at that very moment. While his big brother might think he was an idiot, he'd still cover Chase's ass.

His old man whirled and stabbed him with a glare as he threw the cell phone to the table. "You believe you're so smart, Chasen. We'll see how far you are willing to take this farce when I call a board meeting to have you ousted as CEO."

Chase didn't believe he was smart—he knew. Even so, the threat wasn't idle, but he could hold his own with the board. He'd taken Barron Entertainment from owning one hotel and three media outlets—print, television and radio—to a multibillion-dollar corporation with multiple five-star properties, an entire network of media companies and huge dividends for the very small pool of shareholders. Like all things under the Barron umbrella, the company was family held. That meant his brothers and cousins. They liked the money he made them.

"Well?" Cyrus prodded.

Chase squeezed Savannah's hand as he morphed his expression into one of bored amusement. "Well, what? Which of those nonquestions do you want me to answer?"

"Don't be flip with me, boy."

He bristled, the feeling unsettling. Everyone thought

Cord was the easygoing brother, but Chase was the one who always went with the flow. Until now. "I'm not bein' flip, Dad. Just asking for clarification."

His father stared at him for a long moment, then another, before flicking his gaze to Savannah. "She worth losin' everything for?"

Without scrutinizing his actions for any deeper meanings, Chase tugged Savannah to him, embraced her and dipped his head to take her lips in a gentle kiss that quickly got heated. One hand went low, pressing her hips into his, while his other arm wrapped around her back. Her breath hitched in her lungs and he felt it in the deepest recesses of his existence. He was in trouble, and at the moment, he didn't care. He liked kissing this woman. Liked it a lot. And he decided then and there to woo her. Her hands-off policy? He fully intended to smash right through that.

The way she responded to his kisses assured him she was not immune to his charm. They were married. Married people made love. Oh, yeah, that was definitely on his agenda. As soon as he could convince her that they could have fun together for the yearlong length of their contract.

He broke the kiss and glanced at Tucker, then at his watch.

"Look, this has been all fun and games but I have a corporation to run, Savvie has a meeting and at some point, I plan to get back to our honeymoon."

Cyrus's eyes narrowed. "What's that supposed to mean?"

"It means that you are in the way, Dad. All of you. Unless you are here on a business matter? My personal life is off-limits. I never agreed to marry Janiece and frankly, if I were her, I'd be embarrassed that my father had to buy me a husband. Or in my case, a wife." Chase stared pointedly at Janiece before returning his gaze to Cyrus. "I'm quite capable of finding my own wife, Dad." He still held Savannah's hand, and he brought it to his lips, brushing a kiss over her knuckles before he continued. "As you can see."

Janiece, her eyes shiny bright with unshed tears, leaned against her father as he ushered her to the door. Mal glowered at Cyrus and muttered, "I've never been so embarrassed. You owe me, Barron." He patted Janiece's back as he said, "We're going home, girl. We're so done with this." They disappeared through the apartment door, slamming it behind them.

Chase faced off against his father, Tucker and Savvie by his side. "This conversation is done, Dad. You want a board meeting? Call it. I'm good at what I do. You know it. You think you can do it better? Go for it. I believe the board won't be very happy with your management style but if you're feeling lucky? No skin off my nose."

"This isn't over, Chasen." Cyrus pivoted, marched to the door, jerked it open and left it gaping after he passed through.

Tucker drifted after him, made sure his uncle had disappeared into his suite across the hall, then shut the door. He turned to face the couple. "Gee, that went well."

Savannah parked her brand-spanking-new Ford truck next to the equally new and shiny horse trailer in the long-term parking area of the Clark County Fairgrounds. She locked up the pickup and sighed as her fingers traced the emblem on the driver's door. What a difference a couple of days made. Shoving the keys into the front pocket of her jeans, she strolled toward the barn where Indigo's stall was located. As she approached, she recognized the silhouette of the big man framed in the doorway.

Her gait slowed and she inhaled deeply several times to settle her nerves. As soon as she was close enough, she noticed the disgruntled expression on Kade's face. He was not happy.

"What the hell were you thinking?" he asked as soon as she was close enough to hear. "Oh, wait. You weren't!"

"Gee. Hi, Kade. Happy to see you, too." She fought the urge to look away while digging the toe of her brand-new boot into the dirt.

"C'mere." He opened his arms, and she fell into them.

"Oh, Kade." She squiggled her nose against the burn of tears, and blinked moisture out of her eyes.

"What's wrong, baby girl?"

"His father."

"Cyrus?"

"Yeah."

"Crap. He's here?"

"Yes. He... Oh, lordy, Kade. That man is just evil. He... The things he said. The threats. Poor Chase."

"Whoa. What? Poor *Chase*?"

She pushed off his chest and backed up a few steps. "That man is despicable."

"Chase?"

"No. His father. Keep up here, Kade." He shook his

head, laughing, and Savvie breathed easier. "Chase is… He's not what I expected."

"What's that mean?" Kade focused on her and she smoothed out her expression.

"Later. Show me who you brought me?"

"No, sooner, but I'll let it go for now, hon. C'mon." He turned on his heel and headed into the shadowy barn. "I checked Indy. I think he'll be okay after treatment and rehab. He'll get both at the Crown B."

The band around her chest eased a little as she caught up to the man who was essentially her big brother—chosen by her heart, not by shared blood. "I was really worried, Kade. That's good."

He snagged her hand and squeezed, but didn't let go as he led her toward the stalls at the end of the long aisle. "You're gonna tell me all about the wild hair you got, but first…" Kade stopped at a stall.

A black-and-white paint quarter horse dropped his head over the gate and nickered softly. Her heart melted as she gazed into the horse's big brown eyes. "Well, howdy there, handsome."

"This is Barron's Cimarron River, Sav. He's your new barrel racer."

She rubbed her knuckles against the horse's forehead and he arched his neck to make it easier for her to reach.

"I should warn you, the beast is spoiled rotten. Miz Beth took a shine to him and snuck him carrots when I wasn't looking. He's especially fond of the baby variety."

That made Savannah laugh. "I'll be sure to carry a supply."

"That new trailer will make it easy. It's got a fridge in the dressing area."

"Yeah. I know." Savvie glanced over her shoulder. "Kade—"

"Not now. We'll sit down. Talk. Business first."

"Okay."

"Now, this fellow…" He pulled her away from Cimarron and nudged her toward the next stall. "This is Barron's Red River."

The horse that arched his head over the stall door was the color of his name—a bloodred sorrel with a slightly darker mane and tail. Savvie stroked his nose as Kade continued. "Big Red's a worker. And he's smart. You point him at a calf, he knows what to do. Team roping, he'll go either way like I said, but he's a better header."

She moved to stroke the horse's muscular neck. "Good to know." When team roping, one rider roped the steer's horns, and only the horns. There was a time penalty for catching the cow around the neck. The second rider basically dropped a loop on the ground to catch the steer's rear feet—his heels. Again, there was a penalty for catching only one hoof. "I prefer to head so it's all gravy."

"You found a partner yet?"

Glancing over her shoulder, she studied the man she'd known since she was a toddler. "Been a little busy."

"Yeah. Figured."

"Kade…"

"Later, babe. Where's your saddle? It's going in the trash."

"What?"

"Your tack is crap, Sav. I know that. You know that. Tucker told me to get the best. I went to The Saddlery in Cowtown. Rusty knows you so you now have the best. Saddles aren't quite custom fitted but close. I have a gear kit put together, too. S'already in your trailer. Let's get these boys saddled and exercised."

A grin split her face. As far as she was concerned, a bad day on a horse was better than a good day anywhere else. Except… Chase's kisses were pretty darn good. She caught a flash of dull gold on her left hand and looked down. Her fake wedding band. Her feelings dampened a bit. Yeah. The fake jewelry that left a dark band, as she'd discovered when she washed her hands, was symbolic of her fake marriage. It didn't matter that Chase was handsome. Funny. Charming. And could kiss. This was a business deal. And it was time to get down to business.

Nine

Chase needed to keep his thoughts on the business at hand. The Carrolls had checked out and returned to Oklahoma. His father was still occupying the suite across the hall. Chase had had Tucker change the security codes and fire the desk clerk who'd given his father access. From that moment on, no one got a card key to the apartment unless the order came directly from Chase or Tucker. It didn't matter who made the request. His hotel, his rules.

Savannah had gone to the fairgrounds to meet Kade, and Chase's thoughts kept wandering to the woman he'd taken as a bride. She surprised him. Continuously. He liked that. A lot.

He heard a throat being cleared. Tucker nailed his shin under the table. He jerked.

"What?"

"We cutting into your daydreams, Chase?"

He glared at his cousin before turning his gaze to the two businessmen from the United Arab Emirates. "I'm sorry, gentlemen. I admit my mind is elsewhere."

The two men exchanged knowing glances. "We understand congratulations are in order, Mr. Barron. I must admire a man who would leave his marriage bed to take care of business."

Okay, he could work with this. "I have a most understanding wife and as this meeting was already scheduled, I did not want to inconvenience you."

Chase glanced toward the architect and nodded. The man and his assistant rose, grabbed a cardboard tube and emptied it. In moments, the conference table was covered with floor plans and three-dimensional drawings. The Arab hoteliers were suitably impressed with the concept for the hotel and resort complex Barron Entertainment wanted to build in Dubai. This was Chase's project. One his father didn't know about. One that would make him and the company a desertful of money. He sat back in his chair, letting the artistic types use all the adjectives.

Catching Tucker's eye, he allowed a tiny twitch to curl the right side of his mouth into a hidden smile. His cousin's left eye lowered halfway. Yeah, they were on the same page and it felt good. Tuck always had his back, had since they were kids and thick as thieves. Chase, Cash, Tucker and Bridger Tate. The four musketeers. Now Bridge worked with Cash the way Tuck worked with him.

He made a note to call Cash to discuss the recent security breaches on the Crown's casino floor. His instincts screamed there was something more about the situation, but he couldn't put his finger on what troubled him. Security was Cash's baby. Chase felt secure in handing over the problem to his twin.

The Arabs were asking questions now. He continued to observe them, the nuances of their words, the exchanged glances and subtle body language. Oh, yeah. He had them hook, line and sinker. He'd get their signatures on the bottom line. Business first and then he'd track down his wife and commence with Operation Seduce Savannah.

Savannah, mounted on Cimarron, raced across the arena. Dirt flew behind the horse's hooves. Her heels rubbed Cim's sides, urging more speed. She kept her hands soft, the reins flapping against his neck. Then she pulled the big paint to a sliding stop with the barest lift and tug on the reins. The horse's mouth was just as sensitive as Kade had implied. She could work with that.

Easing the big animal around, she rode to the spot where Kade leaned against the fence, stopwatch in his hand.

"Well?"

"Thirteen point five." He grinned at her. "You'd be in the money with that time. Not bad, Sav. Not bad at all."

She grinned back, the smile so big her cheeks crinkled. "He has more to give, Kade. A lot more. Look at him!" She leaned forward and patted the horse's neck. "He's not even breathing hard. I can get under thirteen. Heck, I might even break twelve!"

"Yeah, I think you might." Kade reached through

the fence and teased Cim's chin. "Let's get him cooled down and put up. I'm hungry. I'll buy you lunch."

Sav raised her arm to check her watch. "Two? It's already two o'clock? Dang. Yeah, I'm starved, too."

She urged Cim toward the gate and Kade met her there, opening then closing it behind her. She swung down from the saddle, loosened the girth and led the paint back to the barn, Kade keeping pace with her.

Before she could strip the saddle, Kade had already done so. While he carried it out to her trailer, she curried the horse, crooning to him and promising to bring carrots. Movement at the stall door caught her attention.

Kade braced his forearms on the top of the gate and watched her. She kept brushing, knowing he'd speak his mind sooner than later. He didn't disappoint.

"He's a player, Sav."

"Duh, Kade. I read when I'm standing in line at the grocery store."

"The headlines don't say it all."

"He's a Barron. That pretty much says the rest." It did, but it didn't. It didn't say Chase could be as sweet as he was clueless. It didn't say that the man could curl her toes with a kiss. It didn't say that now, after seeing Kade, Chase and old Mr. Barron up close, she could see what her mother saw. If Kade wasn't a Barron, there'd been gene splicing in his mother's womb.

"Have you two had sex?"

"Kade!" Heat rushed into her cheeks and she knew she was blushing furiously. "That is none of your business."

"I repeat, hon. Player."

"And I repeat, bro. I know. We have an agreement. This is a business arrangement."

"I've stayed in his apartment, Sav. He doesn't have a guest room."

"No. But."

"But what?"

"His bed is huge."

"And?"

"And I sleep on one side, he sleeps on the other." At least she hoped he did. She'd been passed out drunk last night and couldn't remember. Janiece's shrill voice had been such a shock to her system, Savvie didn't stop to consider things when she first opened her eyes. She'd woken up alone. That said volumes. Or so she thought.

"Hon, Chase attracts woman troubles like honeysuckle draws bees."

"I'm not sure of that, Kade." She reviewed what she thought she knew about Chase, and the things he'd said in passing. "I think maybe that sometimes he—"

"Sometimes I what?" Chase appeared next to Kade at the stall door and Savvie blushed.

"Y'all wanna explain why I'm the topic of conversation?" Chase was pissed.

Kade turned his head and gave him a lazy once-over before returning his attention to Sav.

"Didn't expect to see you out here, Chase. I thought you had a meeting," Savvie said.

"Had a meeting, babe. Now I'm here. Anything wrong with wanting to see my wife?" Her eyes widened and she opened her mouth to speak, but he cut her off. "Our business is our business, Savannah. You don't discuss it with employees."

Her nostrils flared, and her face colored beyond her previous blush. "Excuse me? You know what Kade is to me. And come to think of it, what am I? I'm your employee, too."

Chase felt Kade shift beside him, but he kept his gaze focused on Savannah. He liked that she had a temper. He liked that she was loyal, but she should be loyal to him, not... Chase cut that thought off. She considered Kade her family. After overhearing Sav's conversation with her mother that morning, he could understand why she was angry. While he should be thankful Kade was looking out for her, he was still pissed. She should be turning to him for that support. He was her husband. Only...not. She was right about that, too.

Chase reined in his emotions. What was it about this woman that sent him reeling from one extreme to another? He wimped out and completely changed the subject. "Good-lookin' horse, Kade."

The man beside him snorted. "Your cousin told me to bring the best."

He cut his eyes to Kade, then returned his gaze to Savvie. "I came to see if you wanted to go to lunch with me."

"No. I'm busy," she replied.

"Sav." The way he said her nickname got two pairs of eyes snapping to him.

"I'm doing lunch with Kade."

"He can join us."

"No."

"Sav." Chase said it again and gave her The Look. He recognized the moment she wavered, and pressed his point. "We'll take your new truck. You can drive."

He was so intent on her reactions, he missed Kade shifting away and turning to face him.

"Yeah, Sav. Let's do lunch with the boss."

Chase watched Savannah's gaze dart between him and Kade. One part of him wondered what Kade was up to, while the other was glad the man appeared to agree with him. "We'll go to Cantina Del Sol."

"Is that where we ate the other day?"

Yup, he knew the way to her forgiveness. Food. "Yeah."

"Okay."

"Okay."

Chase ended up driving. She rode shotgun, but spent the trip twisted around in her seat talking to Kade. Every time Chase glanced at the rearview, Kade's eyes met his in the mirror. He and Kade would need to come to a meeting of the minds much sooner than later.

As he drove, Savvie filled the other man in on their arrangement, finishing with "So see? I'm not being dumb, Kade. I thought it through." She reached around her seat to grasp his hand. "Mom doesn't get to win. Not this time. And it's important to me. I've wanted the chance to compete on this level since I won my first belt buckle. You know that, Kade. You were sitting there on the fence cheering me on."

"Savvie, you were ten, and it was a kid's rodeo."

"And now I'm twenty-five. I had a good shot with Indigo. A really good shot. I got my hands on him by a fluke and a lot of horse trading. I have to stand on my own two feet."

As Chase watched in the mirror, Kade's tan skin darkened. "Your own two feet? How are you doin' that, baby girl? Chase is payin' your bills. Giving you the ways and means. What's he expect in payment?"

Before Chase could jump in to defend his actions, Savvie released Kade's hand and caught his. "Get your mind out of the gutter, Kaden Waite. You know me. We…" She gestured between herself and him before continuing. "Chase and me have an agreement. A contract. It's business. He gets advertising. I get a sponsorship."

"Then why are you married?"

"Because it was expedient," Chase interjected after a pause.

He didn't say anything else as he pulled into a parking lot and maneuvered the big vehicle into a pair of spaces. He retrieved Savannah's hand and twisted in the driver's seat so he could see both Sav and Kade.

"The old man was setting me up to get married, Kade. He even dragged Janiece Carroll and her father out here to force an engagement. Savannah needed a sponsor. I needed a wife. We have a prenup. She's covered. She'll get what she wants. This time next year, I'll do something stupid to give her grounds for divorce. She walks away with this truck, the trailer, all the gear you brought, plus the three horses. If she's as good as I think she is, she'll also have the All-Around Cowgirl Championship buckle, trophy and winnings. She walks away with two hundred and fifty thousand dollars over and above what I spend on her expenses. It's all a win for her."

"Except for spending nights in your bed."

Chase bit back a retort. Now was not the time to lose his temper, but Savannah beat him to a reply.

"He hasn't touched me, Kade. That's part of the

contract. Yes, in public we act like newlyweds and a happily married couple. That's a show for his father."

"A show for Cyrus? Dammit, Savannah, do you know what this makes you? A frickin' gold digger. I never thought—"

"Shut up, Kaden." Chase's voice was pure icy anger. No one disrespected Savannah. Especially not the man she considered family. "Nobody says that crap about Savannah. No one, not even you. My father stood there in my home—*our* home—this morning, a checkbook in his hand. You want to know what Savannah told him? She got toe-to-toe right up in his face and told him he didn't have enough zeroes to buy her off. She is *not* a gold digger, and you damn well will never say anything bad about her. Ever. You got me?"

Kade settled back against the seat, his gaze fixed on Chase. Emotion flickered across his expression, but Chase couldn't read its meaning.

"Okay, then."

Chase narrowed his eyes. "What's that mean?"

"You're right. I need to trust Savvie."

Chase jerked his chin down in acknowledgment. "Okay, then."

Ten

Kade stayed through Saturday. He was there cheering Savannah on, helping her with the horses and watching. Always watching. Before her runs on Saturday night, she approached him as he saddled Big Red for the roping event.

"Hey." She touched his arm and made sure she had his total attention. "I know what I'm doing."

"Does Chase?"

Kade's question threw her off stride. "What do you mean?"

"I see the way he looks at you, Savvie. He wants you."

His assertion should not have made her feel the way it did. She should not feel giddy and all, *OMG, he likes me!* Pushing those thoughts away, she considered Kade's statement and what she knew of Chase. He likcd women. *Lots* of women. She was just one more notch on his bedpost. Right? Right! As long as she remembered that, she'd suffer through those searing kisses of his and resort to cold showers.

"I'm female, Kade. I'm not totally clueless, but we have an agreement. And I'll be gone first thing Monday morning. He's putting on a show for the cameras and his family. That's all."

Her best friend growled under his breath as he backed away to shake out her rope, removing the twists before looping it and dropping it over the saddle horn. She would not back down on this.

"Do you trust me?"

His head whipped around, and his sharp gaze stabbed her. "What kind of question is that, Sav?"

"The one you're forcing me to ask. Answer me."

"Of course I do."

"Then trust me. I know Chase. Yes, he's a player, but let's face it. I am *not* his type."

"You're female. That makes you his type."

She snorted out a laugh, catching Kade off guard if his scowl was any indication. "Hon, trust me. I am *not* his type. I don't have long legs, I have thunder thighs. I don't have melons, I have grapefruit. All my curves went south. He likes them runway thin, blonde and high maintenance. I am definitely not any of those things."

Kade stared at her for a long moment. "You don't have a clue, Savannah." He made a sweeping gesture with his hand. "There isn't a guy within a mile radius who wouldn't jump on you if you offered."

Sav rocked back on her heels, shocked but pleased. "Really?"

Tilting his head back, eyes to heaven, Kade sighed heavily. "You are clueless, babe. Totally clueless." He lowered his chin to look at her. "Yes. Really. You have any idea how many horny football players I beat up in high school?"

She giggled, then clapped her hand over her mouth. "No. You didn't!" At his slow nod, she bit her lips to get control before she continued. "No wonder I didn't have a date for prom."

"You had a date."

"With you! Not cool, Kade. You're like my brother." She rolled her eyes and curled her lip into a disgusted snarl even as she fought laughter.

"Yeah. I am. And that's why we're having this conversation." He rubbed the back of his neck, then dropped a hand to her shoulder to get and keep her attention. "Look, I understand why you're doing this. I do. I don't like the way you're doing it, but I understand. Still, I'm worried. The guy is bad news. All the Barrons are." Some delayed emotion drifted across his features. "Well, the twins are. The others? They found good women, changed. But Chase and Cash? Not good, babe. Not good at all."

Chase stood close enough to hear their conversation, but was hidden in shadow. He should be angry that his employee was talking to Savannah and saying the things he said. At the same time, he was well aware of his reputation—one he'd somewhat fostered. One that was coming back to bite him in the ass now. He'd discovered something over the past several days spent with Savannah. He liked her. As a person. Granted, he found her sexy and enjoyed kissing her far more than he should, given the circumstances, but he was male. And she was very, *very* female. In all the right places.

He wasn't upset that Kade noticed, or that other men noticed how attractive Savannah was. As long as none of them tried to act on their urges and as long as she rebuffed them. She was Chase's wife. She had to stay beyond reproach to keep his old man off his back. At the same time, he was a little irate that Kade thought so little of him. He'd never done anything to Kade. None of his brothers had. The ranch foreman carried the Barron stamp, whether the guy knew it or not. Cyrus would never acknowledge an illegitimate son, which sucked for Kade, but Chase and his brothers had always treated him with respect. To find out now, under these circumstances, that Kade had so little respect for him stung.

The loudspeaker announced the next event—calf roping. He'd come back behind the chutes to wish Savannah good luck. She'd had good barrel racing runs and he thought she'd done okay with the calf roping so far, though she didn't have the best times. He didn't want to give away the fact he'd overheard them, so he faded farther back into the shadows and made his way to the box seat he'd bought. He'd managed to duck the gaggle of paparazzi they picked up every time they left the hotel, by slipping into the men's room. The photogs hadn't done their homework. There was a back exit that led to the competitors-only area.

Photos and stories were hitting the entertainment sites, along with tweets and Facebook postings. His cell phone had blown up with texts and voice mails. He was careful about sharing his number with most women, but a few had it. They were upset. He'd never made promises to them, nor had he thought about choosing any of them to get him out of this situation. Savannah had been in the right place at the right time, and she was the right woman.

Stopping at the concession stand, he grabbed a beer and returned to his seat. He sipped and reflected while waiting for Savannah's name to be called. The last couple of nights had been sheer torture. The night of their wedding, when she was so cutely drunk, Savvie had rolled into his side, snuggled in with her head on his shoulder and her arm draped across his bare chest. He tended to sleep nude but had kept his part of the bargain by wearing cotton sleep pants. She'd worn a tank that hid nothing and soft pants that slipped low on her hips.

He'd spent the whole night half-awake and totally aroused. Still, he'd kept his promise. He hadn't taken advantage. Once upon a time, he might have. Savannah had sought him out, wanting to sleep close. That said something about her feelings. But taking advantage of her hadn't been in the cards. She trusted him. Oh, he fully planned to seduce her, to make love to her, but he'd do it when she was sober—well, mostly sober. If she had a few beers or some wine to mellow out? He could work with that.

Thursday and Friday night she'd scrupulously stayed on her side of his California king bed. In a T-shirt. A long-sleeved T-shirt. And socks. He slept hot and tended to keep the room cooler at night, but her getup was ridiculous, and they both knew it was a futile attempt to keep him at bay.

He was so lost in his thoughts, he almost missed the announcer. "Here's a real show of dedication, folks.

Next competitor is Savannah Wolfe Barron. She might
be on her honeymoon but she's a real cowgirl because
here she is."

That comment would generate more tweets and In-
stagrams and news reports. Still, it fit the narrative he
was building. Chase could live with the publicity, and
he figured it wouldn't hurt Savannah's quest for the
National Finals.

The calf burst from the chute and a second later, Savannah followed on Big Red. The sorrel was right on
top of the calf in a few strides. Sav dropped her lasso
over the animal's head, her arm whipping back to snug
the loop as she twisted the rope around her saddle horn.
Red slid to a stop even as Sav stepped from the saddle,
dashed to the calf, grabbed, grounded and snugged in
three legs while she tied them with the pigging string
she'd carried in her mouth. She threw her arms up and
the air horn sounded.

From the cheers, he figured she'd gotten a good
time. He really needed to bone up on rodeo events.
Sooner or later, some nosy reporter would ask. Plus,
with Operation Seduce Savannah in full force and effect, he needed the edge so he could celebrate and
compliment her achievements.

After the calf roping ended, he headed back to the
contestant area. He'd take Savannah to a late dinner,
take her home. There would be a hot bath. Maybe wine.
The offer of a massage for tired muscles. He gave good
rubdowns. Women enjoyed his hands.

He found Sav and Kade in the barn, rubbing down
the horses. He pitched in, putting out feed and hay,
then carrying her saddles back to the trailer and lock-

ing it up. To be nice, he offered to include Kade in his dinner plans.

"Thanks, but no. I'm leaving at the butt crack of dawn, and I've got to swing by here to load Indigo before I go."

A look of concern washed over Savannah's face, and she focused on the stall where the black horse was stabled. Kade squeezed her shoulder.

"He'll be fine, Sav. I'll take care of him."

She offered Kade a tentative smile that seared Chase right down to his core. "I know you will. I just…" She drifted toward Indigo and the horse reacted by arching his head over the gate. Savvie rubbed his cheek and ears. "He's been good to me. I'll miss him."

Without thinking, Chase closed the distance between them and reached for her. He tugged her close for a hug. "I'll make sure Indy gets whatever he needs. And if you want to fly in to see him while you're on the road, do it. I'll cover the expense."

He physically felt Kade's stare burning into his back and raised his head to stare back. Chase was staking his claim, showing that Savannah's feelings were important to him, declaring that he understood what was important to her.

"I… Wow, Chase. That's…"

He returned his attention to the woman in his arms. "Shh. If you get the urge, fly home, kitten. Rent a car or I'll have someone pick you up at the airport." He glanced back to Kade. "Pretty sure Kade won't mind meeting you. You can stay in my room at the ranch. Though, fair warning. Miz Beth is nosy." He chuckled and felt Savvie's arms slip around his waist.

"I can handle Miz Beth."

He laughed outright at that. "I know you can, honey." He leaned back a little so he could see her face. "You can handle anything and everything, Savannah."

Eleven

After parting ways with Kade in the parking lot, Savannah folded into the passenger seat of Chase's Jaguar. She waited until he was settled and buckling his seat belt before speaking.

"I can drive the truck back to the hotel, you know. So you don't have to get up early and bring me back out here tomorrow morning."

"Kitten."

Those two syllables held layers of nuance and hidden meanings. "How do you do that?"

He glanced at her, amusement gleaming in his eyes. "Do what?"

"Guys. How do guys put so much into so little?"

He started the sleek vehicle, shifted into Reverse and backed out of the parking space. "I'm not following you, kitten."

"See? You did it again."

This time he laughed as he drove out of the lot. "Still not making sense."

"Men seldom do." She huffed a breath that ruffled the hair curving across her forehead. "Say it again."

"Say what?"

"Kitten."

She knew he was humoring her when he said it. "Kitten."

"See?"

"No, babe, I don't. Care to enlighten me?"

"Doesn't matter that it's only two syllables. When you say it—depending on how you say it—it says so much."

"Okay…" Chase drew out the word.

"I see you aren't following. Or maybe you are and there's some secret guy code that prevents you from explaining."

"Okay."

"Again! One word. And the way you said it just now makes it have completely different meanings."

"Okay."

"Stop it!" She slapped at his biceps and his laughter curled around her heart.

"I think I'm following. Sort of."

"Look, the first time you said *kitten*, there was a wealth of meaning there."

"What did I mean when I said it the first time?"

"I was making the point that you could sleep in rather than drag your butt out of bed to drive me out to the fairgrounds. Rodeo isn't your thing. There's no sense in you hanging around all day. So I say that.

And you say *kitten*." She did her best to emulate the way he'd said it.

"And?"

"And what you said was that you were going to get up early, drive me out to the fairgrounds and hang around all day. That you *expected* to get up early, drive me and hang out. And that I should expect you to expect that."

"I said all that?"

"Well…yeah. Didn't you?"

"Sort of. What I actually said was that I'm a guy, I drive, you're my girl, so I'm going to drive you. And I'm expected to do those things and hang out all day because we just got married, are ostensibly on our honeymoon and that's what's expected of a newly married couple."

"See? That's exactly it. You said all that in a two-syllable word. A pet name. It's…" She sighed. "How do guys do that?"

He laughed again, but she didn't think he was laughing at her. He was simply enjoying the conversation. "Aren't guys supposed to be the strong, silent types?" She caught his glance and nodded. "So we have to learn to communicate in as few words as possible."

"Well, you do it well."

He offered her a three-quarter profile, an arched brow and a smug smile. "I do everything well."

"I've heard that." That got her a dimpled smile, which sent a little quiver shooting through her.

"You hungry?"

Savannah wanted to throw her hands in the air in frustration. Two words. Two innocuous words. He was asking if she'd like to get something to eat. She would.

Her stomach was about a minute away from growling. But she wasn't thinking about food. She was thinking about him. And doing things to him. Him doing things to her. So yeah, she was hungry.

"I could eat."

That got her a sideways glance. "Want to go out or head home and order room service?"

She should remain in public with him. Definitely. "Let's do room service. I need a shower."

And dang if that didn't get her a full-face look and a slow, sexy grin. What was she thinking? And why wasn't her mouth obeying her brain?

"I can work with that."

Wisely keeping her mouth shut, she remained silent until they got to the hotel, rode up in the elevator and entered his apartment.

"Trust me?"

His question caught her off guard, and she gave him a narrow-eyed look. "Yeah…"

"Go grab your shower. I'll order up dinner."

"And what does any of that have to do with trust?" Oh, but he was devilish when his eyes twinkled like that. She breathed in deeply.

"Trust me to order something you'll like."

She wasn't expecting that answer, and she blinked a few times in order to catch up. "Oh. Uh, sure."

He flashed another smile, this one with only a hint of dimple, before he gripped her shoulders, turned her around and nudged her toward the hallway leading to the bedroom and master bath. "Take your time. In fact, if you'd like a bubble bath or—"

A snorting giggle escaped before she could smother

it. "Uh, thanks, but I'm not really a bubble bath kind of girl."

He paused a couple of beats before he said, "That's too bad."

Oh, double dang damn. The way he uttered those words made her want to be that kind of girl—to be girlie and sexy and the type of woman Chase would take to his bed and do really sexy things with.

Chase watched her, doing his best to hide his smile. He'd seen her hesitation, and he couldn't help but notice the sudden added sway to her lush hips as she walked away. Definitely time to put his plan in action. He liked women. Understood them better than a lot of men. Savannah didn't want to be a notch on his bed. She wasn't. They were together for the next year. Married. Married people had sex. He'd make it good for her. Make her happy. Until it was time to make her unhappy so their split looked real.

A twinge of conscience nudged him, but he stuffed it away. Time for food and frolic. He wanted this woman. The more he got to know her, the more he wanted her. She knew who he was. What he was. She'd still signed on the dotted line. Was he cheating with this plan to get her in his bed for something more than sleep? Maybe. He refused to examine his motives too closely. Savannah Wolfe—Savannah Barron, he reminded himself—was intriguing. He wanted to solve the mystery of her, find out what made her tick. Find out what made her moan and beg, made her whisper his name in need.

Forty-five minutes later, he knocked on the closed— and locked—bathroom door.

"Yeah?"

"Food is on its way up, Sav."

"Be right out."

He'd taken the forty-five minutes to change clothes, stripping out of jeans, boots and Western shirt and getting comfortable in sweats and a T-shirt. This was his normal attire for a night in. Mostly. He was dressed as much for comfort as seduction. Wearing those sweats commando made stripping down easy.

Savannah strolled into the living area just as room service knocked on the door. She wore cotton drawstring pants and a slouchy pullover shirt with a wide neck. A spaghetti strap peeked out. Good. She was wearing the camisole tank she normally slept in. He liked the looks of her in that camisole. A lot.

"Grab me a beer, hon?" he called over his shoulder as he answered the door.

Ushering the waiter in, Chase waved him toward the couch and coffee table. "Set up there."

"Sure thing, Mr. B."

Something about the waiter's demeanor tripped alarms, and Chase watched him closely. It took a moment, but he found the miniature video camera the waiter hadn't hidden very well under the lapel of his jacket. Chase had his phone in his hand, texting Security while the guy off-loaded—rather clumsily— the service trolley. The fake waiter made another mistake when he held out the ticket for Chase's signature. Savannah hadn't come out of the kitchen yet and was still out of sight. The guy was lingering to catch a glimpse of her. That was good. It meant Security would be at the door when he walked out.

Chase's phone pinged. Security was in place, so Chase opened the door and shoved the paparazzo out.

The man would be banned from all Barron properties. He'd be marched down to the security office, the
camera footage erased. He'd be photographed, turned
over to Las Vegas police and charged with trespassing.

When Savannah joined Chase, carrying two beers,
she had no idea their privacy had been invaded. At
some point, he'd need his security people to give her a
briefing. Perhaps he should assign a bodyguard. He'd
think on that. He didn't want to scare her, but he didn't
want the tabloids getting too close. For now, though,
it was all about beer, finger food he could feed her
and then far more intimate pursuits. Chase had defi-
nite plans for his bride, and those plans meant she'd
not only be sleeping in his bed, but she'd be *sleeping*
with him. In other words, sleep didn't enter into the
equation at all.

She settled into the deep cushions of his couch—
close but not close enough to suit him. Still, he couldn't
push. Wouldn't, truthfully. It was important she want
him as much as he wanted her. He had a clue she did,
given her reactions every time he kissed her. He enjoyed her breathless sigh when he broke off a kiss,
the quick tensing of muscles before she relaxed into
his embrace.

Putting his plan into motion, he filled a plate with
cheese, crackers, meat and fruit. Leaning back into the
soft leather of his couch, he held out a bite of sharp
cheddar cheese. "Open up, kitten."

Her expression was distrustful. "I can feed myself."

"So?"

"So… I can feed myself."

He schooled the smile wanting to crease his cheeks

and tickled her lips with the point of the cheese wedge.
"Take a bite."

She opened her lips and nibbled at the cheese before
her jaw unclenched, and she allowed him to feed her. It
wasn't wedding cake, but he got a thrill from feeding
her. As she chewed and swallowed, he picked a slice
of green apple. He took a bite, swallowed—crunchy
tart with a hint of sweet. Then before she knew what
he was doing, he kissed her. As he'd anticipated, the
two flavors mixed on their tongues.

Her sharp inhalation caused one breast to collide
with his arm. He cupped her jaw in his palm, caressing her cheek with his thumb. She watched him, her
expression slightly dazed.

"What are you doing?" she whispered, her lips remaining parted and wet from his kiss.

"What does it look like I'm doing?"

"Chase."

Man, but the sound of his name sighing between
those full lips of hers set him on fire. "Not gonna lie
here, kitten. I want you. A lot. We're married. We sleep
in the same bed. I'm yours for the next year. You're
mine." He kissed the tip of her nose before shifting
back a few inches so he could watch her without his
eyes crossing. "Gonna be honest. I had every intention
of keeping our bargain, of not touching you. But, baby?
I gotta say, you're driving me crazy. You're beautiful.
You're sweet. Waking up with you in my arms the
other morning was…" Was what? he wondered. Perfect? Yes. Wonderful? Yes. Something he wanted more
of? Most definitely. But he was not about to admit any
of that to her.

He kissed her again, one arm slipping around her

back, the other holding her head until she sank into the kiss. His hand dropped to her shoulder, then trailed lower to skirt the swell of her breast. When she sighed into his mouth, he moved to cup her, thrilled that the nipple under his fingers pebbled when she pressed into him.

"Bed," he murmured. "Want you in bed."

When she didn't argue, he sat up, taking her with him, then pushed off the couch, holding her cradled in his arms. He didn't quite run to the bedroom, but he was full speed ahead until he dropped onto the huge king, keeping her in his arms.

"Birth control?" he demanded, hoping she was on the pill. He wanted to take her bareback. He was clean and as he throbbed with the need for her, he didn't want to bother with a condom.

"No."

He inhaled around the breath he'd been holding.

"I…" She swallowed, and he got lost watching her throat. "I haven't dated in a while."

What? He didn't care if she had…oh. A part of his brain kicked in. Sort of. In her shy way, she was admitting she'd had no man in her bed. But no pill meant he needed to suit up. As he grew harder and his craving for her grew more intense, he almost forgot why it mattered. He rolled over her, jerked out the drawer in the nearest nightstand, grabbed a handful of foil packets.

"We're good." He wanted her and wanted her now, but he took the time to keep them both safe. Now naked and protected, he moved back over her.

In a long, slow movement, he rolled her onto her back. He kissed the soft hollow where her jaw met her throat. Trailing his lips down the slim column, he kissed his way along her collarbone. His hands skimmed up along her side and removed first her pullover shirt and then her camisole. Impatient at the sight of her breasts, rising and falling with her quickened breath, he stripped off her pants and panties. He pushed his thigh between hers, tangling their legs before settling between hers, his erection pressed against the heat at the V of her thighs. He could see her now, the shape of her face, the gleam in her eyes. He slid into her, and there was a quick hitch of her breath, followed by a slow exhale as he remained buried deep inside.

The moment stretched as he held still, watching her, waiting. Her eyes, at first wide and shocked, softened. Her expression followed, her lips curling at the corners, her jaw relaxing. He had her now. Had almost all of her. Before the night was done, he'd have everything.

He pulled back, watched her eyes narrow, hid his smile as her inner muscles clutched at him, working to keep him inside. He gave her what she wanted, pushing back in. Her eyes widened again, then her lashes fluttered closed to paint half-moon shadows on her high cheekbones.

"Don't." He murmured the entreaty. "Look at me, kitten. I want to see your eyes."

She did as he requested, hesitantly, her skin tingeing with embarrassment.

"Don't." An order this time. "This is just us, Savannah. Just you. Just me. Nobody intrudes here but us. You're beautiful. This is beautiful."

"I…" She swallowed hard, not finishing the sentence.

He watched her throat work, thinking of her mouth, and the part of his body currently buried inside her.

That would come later. There were all sorts of things he wanted to do to and with this woman. She swiveled her hips, and he forgot to think at all.

Long, slow and deep. Over and over again. In. Out. He held her gaze, studied her, devoured the range of emotions disclosed there. Her body was rising toward him, his falling toward hers. She shuddered and groped for his hands. Their fingers linked, their mouths met, their breaths mingled.

He watched desire suffuse her face, felt his own climax climbing up his spine. "With me, baby," he ordered. "With me."

They exploded together, and the look in her eyes undid him as he watched. Passion. Need. Want. Hope. Trust. Those last two froze him. What was he doing? This was business. Sex usually was for him, but this woman made him feel things—guilt, contentment, protectiveness. He had no room in his life for those things. Especially not with this woman.

He rolled away to divest himself of their protection. A moment later, he snuggled her in close to his side, her head on his shoulder. "Go to sleep, kitten."

He listened as her breathing deepened, soft puffs of air teasing the hair on his chest. This was good. He liked this. He'd enjoy it tonight and tomorrow would take care of itself.

She was warm and naked, still soft from their lovemaking and sleep. Here in the dark, running his hands over her curves, he wondered if this was a dream. Touch. Fragrance. Sighs in the shadows of his darkened room. Savannah stretched, rolled into him, her lips leaving a damp trail across his skin. Fingers stroked over him, stirring him back to life.

He nudged her to lie across his body, her legs trapped between his. He cupped her face, stared into her eyes, looking for…something. He wasn't sure what. Acceptance? Desire? Maybe even a hint of love. She lowered her head, pushing against his palms. Her mouth sank to his, her body melting around him.

She sighed into the kiss, something wistful in the sound. Or maybe that was him. Maybe he wanted something more from this woman, from this relationship. Something he'd never have, never hoped to have. As she lay over him, he traced the curves of her heart-shaped butt, brushing his fingers up her spine, enjoying the shiver his action invoked. He cupped her shoulders—broader, stronger than those of the women who normally shared his bed. His hands swept down her back, the long, muscular line of it, until his hands once again cupped her. He smiled, remembering how he'd wanted to put his hands in her hip pockets to do just this. Skin to skin was infinitely better.

He hooked the backs of her thighs, repositioned her to straddle him, then reached for a condom. "Ride me, kitten," he commanded, once he was sleeved up.

"Yeah. I like that idea." She pushed off her knees, got him situated and sank down on him. Slow. Oh, so very slow. His hands gripped her thighs, her muscles bunched beneath them, giving her exquisite control. Lots of dirty words swirled in his brain. Crude words for what they were doing. He didn't say them. Not out loud. This moment between them was too divine for the vernacular.

She rode him slow. Rode him hard. Her heart galloped beneath his palm where he cupped her breast. He looked down, watching where their bodies remained connected. It was one of the sexiest sights he'd ever seen. Then his gaze traveled up her body. Golden tan skin, flushed with a tinge of pink. Dark hair tousled and playing peekaboo with her full breasts. Head thrown back, tongue kissing her lips and leaving them moist. He'd been wrong. *This* was the sexiest thing he'd ever seen.

They both came, again at the same time. She collapsed over him, her face buried against his neck and shoulder. He pushed one of her knees until she straightened her leg. Then he rolled them to their sides, holding her close, caressing her back with slow brushes of his fingertips. "Sleep, kitten. Sleep now."

When he awoke, sun teasing his eyes from the partially opened drapes, Savannah was still curled against him, and he liked it. Liked it a lot. Liked it maybe too much.

Twelve

Sunday afternoon, Savannah stood in the rodeo office, check in hand. She'd won all the go-rounds in the barrel racing and placed in the calf roping. Since she was out of practice at roping she was pleased. Kade hadn't lied about Big Red. The horse was cow savvy. The problem had been her inconsistencies with her loop. Well, that and Chase's presence in the stands cheering her on. Friday night. Saturday. Saturday night. And Sunday afternoon. He'd been sitting in a box right behind the chutes, cheering and whistling each time she competed. It had been distracting. But in a good way.

She offered the rodeo secretary a big smile over her shoulder as she pushed open the office door and walked into a barrage of camera flashes. She stopped dead, hand up to cover her eyes, blinking rapidly.

When her vision cleared, she found Twyla Allan, the rodeo queen, draped across the chest of Savannah's husband, posing for photos. The urge to bang her head against the wall was almost overwhelming. Idiot. She was a complete idiot for getting involved with a player who attracted women like Chase did.

Mouth tight but her head high, she attempted to evade the crowd of paparazzi. She got about four feet when Chase looked up and saw her. She was caught flat-footed when Chase disengaged from the sexy woman with her arms around his neck, strode directly to Savvie and folded her into his arms. He laid a big, fat wet one on her mouth, leaving her breathless and clutching at his shoulders when the kiss ended.

"Oh, wow." She blushed when a cocky grin spread across his face. She hadn't meant to say that aloud. Plus, she was supposed to be angry. He'd been flirting with that woman. After making love to her last night. For hours.

"Definitely wow, kitten." Chase murmured the words against her temple after he tipped her Stetson back. "Smile for the camera, darlin'. A few pics, then we're out of here. I'm taking my girl out for dinner to celebrate."

She did as he instructed, curling into his side and smiling as they were peppered with questions about their sudden marriage and other things. Savvie caught a glimpse of Twyla through the crowd. The girl stood on the edge of the group, hands fisted on her hips and an ugly expression on her face. A real beauty queen in her tight jeans and spangly top. Savvie understood why the girl stared daggers her direction. Sav was nothing to write home about.

"Give us another kiss, Chase!" one of the photographers yelled.

Chase obliged, sweeping her backward in a dip. His mouth fused to hers and her pulse galloped. Once again, she had to clutch his jacket front to keep her equilibrium. He held her like that for what seemed an eternity, then just as suddenly brought her back up to a standing position. His arm remained circling her waist—a good thing since her knees quivered to the point she wasn't sure she could stay upright without that assistance.

"Now, y'all forgive us. We're still on our honeymoon, and my girl has to head out in the morning for her next gig. I get one more night to celebrate with her, and we're going to do it up right." Chase winked at the media mob.

With that, he led her across the parking lot to his car and folded her into the passenger seat. He joined her moments later, the Jag purred to life and they drove away.

"Proud of you, babe. You did good," Chase said as he expertly maneuvered the slick car through traffic.

She caught a glimpse of his profile. He looked relaxed, happy and sincere. *Huh.* She felt a little ridiculous for feeling jealous of Twyla earlier.

"Thanks. I…" On impulse, she reached over and touched his thigh with her fingertips. "With Indy hurt, I couldn't have done this without you."

His eyes slid her direction, and the right corner of his mouth ticked up in a smile. "You'd have figured out a way, Savannah."

His faith in her made her feel warm inside. Without thinking, she squeezed the hard muscle beneath his jeans. Since sharing his apartment, she'd caught glimpses of him in various states of undress—not to mention naked. The man was seriously buff.

She reminded herself not to jump off that cliff. As casually as she could, Savvie withdrew her hand, only to have him grab it and wrap his fingers around hers. "Kinda like touching you, kitten."

"Uh…" Her brain went blank and he chuckled, a sound vibrating from deep in his chest all the way to where his hand held hers. "Uh…"

They caught a red light, and as the car idled, he turned to face her. "I surprised you."

"I… Yeah. A little." She inhaled and squiggled her nose and lips as she debated how much to reveal. "Kade's about the only person who ever believed in me. I'm…not used to compliments like that."

"Kitten."

Wow. The nuances in that one word. Kindness. Compassion. Understanding.

The light changed to green. He was still holding her hand, but his eyes were back on traffic, giving her the opportunity to study him. Getting emotionally involved with Chase Barron was a BAD IDEA, all in caps and followed with a whole line of exclamation points. She was better off remembering his public persona—the one she saw on the tabloid covers whenever she went through a checkout line.

No, she really needed to guard against his charm. One year. He'd given her one year. She'd take it to get her life on track, and when he pulled whatever stunt that made him the bad guy and her the injured party, they would divorce. Everyone would feel sorry for her. There was only one problem with that scenario. Chase was setting himself up to be a bad guy, but he wasn't a bad guy at all.

Lost in thought, she didn't realize they'd arrived at the Crown Casino until the doorman opened the passenger door and extended his hand to help her out. Scrambling, she got her feet under her and stood as Chase came around and joined her. He reclaimed her hand and all those warm feelings suffused her again. Until she realized they had an audience: no paparazzi, but tourists wielding cell phones were very much in evidence.

The scrutiny diminished slightly once they arrived in the lobby. Savannah felt her smile slipping, but Chase squeezed her to him with the arm draped around her shoulders. "We'll have dinner. Celebrate. And then we'll go hide upstairs. Sound like a plan?"

She gave him a tentative smile and nodded. "That works. I'm starved."

"Good. Barron House is famous for its steaks."

"Excuse me." A broad-shoulder man stopped in front of them. He wore a tailored suit but looked like he should be wearing army fatigues with bullet bandoliers draped across his shoulders.

"Problem?" Chase asked.

"Yes, sir. Mr. Tate asked me to send you to the security office as soon as you arrived."

Muttering under his breath, Chase dropped his mouth to Savannah's ear. "Gotta take care of this, kitten. Go on over to the restaurant and get seated. Tell the waiter I'll have my usual and I'll join you as quick as I can." He squeezed her shoulders again. "Sorry about this. Business first."

"I understand." She flashed him a tentative smile

and glanced around the palatial lobby, looking for the steak-house entrance.

"Buck will show you the way, Sav."

She glanced at the man who was part of Chase's security staff. He definitely fit his name.

"Drop her off at Barron House before you come up."

"Yes, sir."

As Chase walked away without a backward glance, Savannah offered a shy smile to the big man still standing in front of her. "If you need to get back to work, I can probably find my way—"

Buck cut her off. "Not a problem, Mrs. Barron. If you'll follow me."

Savannah nodded and fell into step as Buck pivoted on his heel and marched through the lobby. Curious glances—some openly unfriendly—followed her. Shoulders square, head up, she did her best to ignore them.

It felt as though they walked several blocks, dodging the casino floor, trailing past the area she nicknamed "Boutique Row" with its high-end shops. They passed several restaurants—a froufrou café featuring French cuisine by some celebrity chef, a family-friendly diner decorated like something from the 1950s and a bar with art deco murals on the walls—before finally arriving at Barron House. Buck took his leave as soon as the entrance was in sight, and with a bit of trepidation, Savannah approached the imposing maître d'.

"Hi," she ventured. "Table for two?"

She got a snooty look and a cold "Do you have a reservation?"

"Uh…not exactly. At least I don't think so." Before she could mention Chase's name, the maître d' gave her a head-to-toe perusal, and she could tell she'd failed miserably.

"We also have a dress code," the man added, his tone snide.

She leaned a little to the side to glance into the restaurant. There were wood-paneled walls, low lights, white tablecloths and red linen napkins. A multisided fireplace blazed in the center of the space, flames leaping behind faceted glass. Waiters in starched white shirts, black leather vests and long black aprons bustled through the room. Women wore little black dresses. Men wore coats and ties.

Swallowing hard, she stammered, "Oh. I—I'll go change. I'm sorry. I didn't know." People seated nearby were starting to stare and murmur to each other.

Pivoting, she ran smack-dab into a warm body—a very warm and very muscular body. Her Stetson flew off her head but a hand grabbed it.

"Everything okay, kitten?" Chase eyed the maître d'. "Joseph, is there a problem with my table?"

"Mr. Barron, sir. I—I didn't know the young woman was with you. She didn't say."

"My wife shouldn't have to say, Joseph."

"Wife?"

The man sounded stunned, and when Savvie took the chance to look at him, his expression said it all. She was hardly the woman anyone would pick out in a crowd as being married to Chase Barron.

"Yes, Joseph. My wife."

The maître d' stepped closer and leaned in, his voice a low murmur as he said, "But the dress code, sir."

Sav stiffened and tried to pull away from Chase. "I'll go change. It's okay. I'm sorry. I've embarrassed—"

"No." Chase tightened his grip. "You won't change and you have nothing to apologize for." He eased back just a hair and tilted her chin up with two gentle fingers. "You're my wife, Savannah. You wear whatever you want wherever you want, especially in my hotel." His eyes searched hers. "Yeah?"

She nodded. She didn't know what else to do. She replied with a breathy, "Yeah."

"Good." He gave her a tight smile as his gaze slid to the officious man standing nearby, wringing his hands. "You will seat us now, Joseph, and you will report to my office first thing in the morning. We'll discuss your status then."

"Yes, sir. Of course, sir. Right this way, Mr. Barron."

They made it maybe five feet into the restaurant. Savannah's cheeks were burning under the stares of the other patrons, when she felt Chase's hand tighten against the small of her back. She froze when he stopped walking.

She glanced up. Cyrus stood there, seething. "Had you married Janiece, we would never suffer this embarrassment, Chasen. Your choice is unsuitable. This... *woman* is not and never will be good enough to be a Barron."

Thirteen

Chase didn't know how to respond so he hesitated. He realized his mistake the moment Savannah backed away. He glared at his father. "I'm not doing this here and certainly not in public. You need to pack up and go back to Oklahoma City, Dad. I'm married. End of discussion."

"No, you aren't. You're playing games, boy. Just like you always do. You don't love that woman. She's a handy piece to warm your bed while you thumb your nose at me. I know what's best for you, for this family."

Chase stepped closer and hissed out an angry whisper. "Keep your voice down. You complain every time I show up in the tabloids. Well, guess what? Every person in this restaurant has a cell phone, and you can bet they're taking our pictures and blasting them out to every social media outlet on the web."

Cyrus smoothed his expression just as he'd smooth a wrinkle in his suit coat. Chase saw his father's eyes flick behind him right before a self-satisfied smile settled on his face.

"It appears your new bride has cut and run. Come and sit down. We'll have dinner. Discuss things."

Glancing over his shoulder, Chase discovered his father was right. Savannah had disappeared. Anger flashed through him. So much for standing up with him. Fine. He shouldn't have expected loyalty from her, despite what they'd shared last night. He'd seen her expression when she'd come out of the rodeo office earlier. He'd explained that Twyla was a former employee, and that when she'd approached, he'd been cordial. It wasn't his fault the paparazzi were hanging around. And as soon as Savannah appeared, he'd disengaged and caught up to her.

The last thing he needed was his father thinking exactly what Chase was thinking. His marriage to Savannah had to appear real and solid. He'd done his bit, but at the first sign of trouble, she'd tucked her tail and run.

"Chasen? Are you coming?"

Fine. He'd sit. Have dinner. He needed to eat, anyway. Savannah could call for room service and hide. Whatever. "Yeah, Dad. Right behind you."

Savannah didn't run. She didn't cry, despite how much she wanted to. She kept her fists clenched at her sides, her chin up and her steps measured. She was so totally embarrassed—mortified, as her college English professor would say—but far too aware of the stares and the security cameras. She would not give the Barron staff any more reason for gossip. Backtracking through the maze of hallways, she finally found the correct bank of elevators. Her control was hanging by a thread. She stabbed the button. Then stabbed again. And again. Jabbing it with her thumb until a hand gentled her frantic motions.

"Easy, hon. Deep breaths."

Tucker stood beside her, partially shielding her from view. When she regained a little control, he led her to the last elevator. He punched in a code on a number pad and urged her on board.

She faced the back wall, chin tucked to her chest, staring at her boots. She couldn't face Tucker. He'd released her hand and turned toward the doors.

"I need to stop by the security office for a moment, then I'll escort you up to the apartment. Okay?"

Not trusting her voice, she lifted her shoulders almost to her ears.

"Savvie?"

She nodded, still unable to speak.

"Okay, hon." The elevator dinged and the doors opened. Tucker turned her and, keeping a gentle hand on her arm, propelled her down a long hallway. She caught enough in her peripheral vision to realize this was one of the executive floors. Tuck halted before a heavy wooden door, and she waited while he punched in another code, then placed his palm against a plate.

Why would the security to the security room be so secure? Her brain was caught on a hamster wheel of confusion—her way of ignoring the ache in her chest and stalling any sort of processing of what had happened downstairs.

The door opened to laughter and a female voice stating, "I mean, really? Wearing boots and jeans was bad enough, but that cowboy hat? The maître d' went off on her and she all but knocked Chase down."

The laughter died away as the people in the room became aware of who stood in the doorway.

Tucker's voice could freeze-dry steaks as he ordered, "Rack up that footage from Barron House for me. Now."

Savannah cringed and turned away. How soon before that footage hit social media? Anger wafted off Tucker in waves as he watched the exchange between Savannah and the maître d'.

His voice was clipped and hard when he ordered, "Erase it." He stood stock-still, and Savannah sensed movement behind her. "I'll be back as soon as I get Mrs. Barron settled. We'll have a little discussion. No one is off duty until I'm done. We clear?"

She heard a few mechanical squeaks, rustling paper, a couple of murmurs, but they exited to dead silence. Tucker kept his arm around her shoulders as he propelled her down the wide hallway back to the elevator. As soon as he punched in the code, the doors whispered open and they stepped in. With a whoosh she felt in her stomach, they shot upward to the penthouse floor. He walked her to the apartment, keyed the door and ushered her inside. He let the door close before he turned her to face him with his hands resting on her shoulders.

"I'm sorry, honey."

"You didn't do anything."

"No. But I will."

"Please, just let it go."

"Not gonna happen, Savannah. One, they disrespected you. I can't allow that to stand. You're Chase's

wife, even under these circumstances. Employees—
especially those who work in our security office—
are given our absolute trust due to the confidentiality
of the situations they often monitor. I will not allow
what they were doing to continue. We clear on that?"

She swallowed around the lump in her throat and
nodded.

"Good. Two, my cousin can be a total and complete jackass."

That shook her out of her stupor. "Please. Just let it
go. We both know this whole thing is a sham. It's just
pretend. He's not really—" Her voice hitched around
the cold knot forming in her chest. She had to focus
on breathing for a moment. "—not my husband." The
words came out in a whisper.

"He should have come after you, Savannah. You're
the one helping him out of a bind." He shook her gently.
"You deserve better."

"Maybe. I gotta go, Tucker. Please. Just let me go."

He hugged her tight and dropped a kiss to the top
of her head. Then he backed up a step and fished in
his jacket pocket. He handed her an envelope. "It helps
when the Barrons own the bank, but I still pulled some
strings to get it here ASAP. Here's a debit card for your
checking account. There's thirty grand in there for
your travel expenses and bills. If you need more, call
me. Anytime, sweetheart. Okay?"

With gentle care, he knuckled her chin up. "*Anytime*. Yeah?"

"Yeah."

"Good luck, Savannah." He didn't wait for her to
reply. He headed for the door and slipped out.

"I'm gonna need it," she murmured. One thought

kept running through her head. *Idiot. Idiot, idiot, idiot. I'm such an idiot.* If she'd been close to a wall or the breakfast bar, she'd bang her head. How could she have *slept* with him? She *knew* what he was. Who he was. Who his father was. And she'd had about enough.

She schlepped to the bedroom, found her duffel and an empty suitcase in the closet. While an outsider might think there was no rhyme or reason to her packing, she was quite methodical. She knew what she needed to take. She'd leave the rest to keep up the charade.

Thirty minutes later, she was getting into the backseat of a cab, after a five-minute fight with the doorman, who insisted he call the hotel's limo. She'd won the argument.

"Where to?" the cabbie asked, looking at her in the rearview mirror.

"Clark County Fairgrounds. Rodeo barn parking lot."

She had just enough cash in her pocket to pay the cabdriver. Kade had loaded up Indigo and left early that morning. She hitched the new trailer to her new truck, loaded her new horses in the trailer and pulled out. The fuel tanks were topped off but she wanted an ATM. She'd need a big chunk of cash before hitting the road, headed south. The San Antonio Stock Show and Rodeo was her next stop.

She located a truck stop on the outskirts of Henderson and pulled in. She could stock up on Diet Cokes, Snickers and salt-and-vinegar potato chips. She hit the ladies' room and ATM, grabbed her drinks and snacks, and got in line to pay. Within ten minutes, she was ready to go. The truck came with one of those fancy navigation systems. She'd punched in her destination, and it spit out her itinerary. Without the trailer, she could probably make the trip to San Antonio in eighteen hours. With the trailer, she'd need to stop and spend the night somewhere. Considering her late start, it would probably be either Phoenix or Tucson. She'd drive until caffeine didn't work any longer, then she'd find a rest stop. She could let the horses out for a bit of exercise, and grab a nap in relative safety.

That's when she had her first epiphany. She now had three hundred dollars in her pocket, thanks to the ATM. She had a debit card tied to a bank account with thirty thousand available. Well, twenty-nine thousand seven hundred. She could afford to stay wherever she wanted. And wasn't that a kick in the seat of her pants.

She merged onto US 93, accelerated to highway speed, set the cruise control and clicked on the radio. The DJ introduced Cole Swindell's "Ain't Worth the Whiskey" and the opening notes filled her truck.

"Ha! The country music gods are smilin' on me tonight," she announced to the empty cab. As soon as Cole started singing, she was singing along. At the top of her lungs. She didn't care that Chase and his father had shown their true colors. It was time for her to move on. All the way to San Antonio. If she got lucky and stayed on the circuit, she could mostly avoid Chase until she sat across from him in some attorney's office signing the divorce papers a year from now. She raised her Coke bottle in a not-so-silent toast, considering she was still singing—only slightly off-key. When the next song came on, Savannah launched into it, as well. The music gods were happy tonight and sending her way every great breakup-he-done-me-wrong song on the playlist.

The lights of Las Vegas faded to a dull glow in her side mirrors. The truck's headlights swept down the highway. This was her life. A million stars overhead, wide-open spaces, good music and the rodeo. To hell with Chase Barron. And his kisses. He'd left her alone after both old man Barron and the maître d' humiliated her. She was done with him. So. Done. So done she ignored the ache in her chest. She knew better than to dream, knew better than to fall for a sweet-talkin' man. She wasn't her mother.

Fourteen

Chase let himself into the apartment quietly. After shutting and securing the door for the night, he breathed in relief. The automatic lights in the living room cast a soft glow. The rest of the place remained shrouded in darkness. He'd hoped Savannah would be there waiting for him.

She wasn't. The couch was empty. So was the kitchen. He didn't bother checking his office. She wouldn't be in there. He headed to the bedroom, a slow smirk appearing. He'd acted like a jerk, but the talk with his father had been worth it. They'd come to an agreement. Of sorts. Barron Entertainment was still his. Cyrus would butt out of his personal life. If he didn't get Savannah pregnant in two years, he'd cut her loose with a small settlement. Since he planned to divorce her in a year that was an easy stipulation to accept.

He felt his way to the bathroom, slipped inside and shut the door before he turned on the light. Once he got into bed, he'd wake Savannah, make love to her by way of apology for all she'd had to put up with tonight, and then they'd have breakfast in the morning before she headed off to…wherever she was off to for her next rodeo appearance.

Chase was halfway through brushing his teeth before he realized his bathroom counter was all but empty. He pulled out drawers. Empty. He looked up in the mirror. The short satin robe Savannah wore was still hanging there. He spit and rinsed, wiped his face and opened the door.

A rectangle of light slanted across the bed. The empty bed. He flicked on the bedside lamp. Her phone wasn't charging on the nightstand. Her boots weren't lined up next to the chair where she sat to put them on in the morning. Chase tore open the closet door. Most of the clothes Tucker had bought for her were still hanging there. He sorted through the hangers carefully. She'd taken a few things. A fringed leather jacket. A couple of skirts. All the jeans. Every pair of boots.

The drawers holding her underwear, T-shirts and sleep stuff were empty. Prowling through the apartment, he flipped on every light in the place. Getting progressively angrier, he searched for a message from Savannah. And found none. What did she think she was doing, running out on him like this? His cell pinged and he dug it out of his pocket. Maybe she'd left him a text. The current text was from Tucker. He ignored it to scroll through messages and emails. Still nothing from Savannah. He swiped his thumb across the screen to load Tucker's message.

Situation in security office. Next time you ignore your wife to have dinner with your old man, try to do it away from cameras.

What the hell? Rather than call Tucker, he stormed out and headed down to the executive floors. Five minutes later, Chase threw the security room door open and stood there with his hands on his hips, not bothering to hide his anger. The people scanning the monitors briefly looked up. With no exceptions, their gazes slid guiltily away. His focus narrowed on Tucker, and four people standing with him, their eyes downcast.

"Tuck?"

"Not now, Chase. I'll brief you shortly."

Someone cleared a throat behind him and Chase glanced back. Four burly security guards stood in the hallway, waiting. He stepped farther into the monitor room to let them enter. Each one escorted out one of the people—two women and two men—who'd been standing with Tucker.

"Short bathroom breaks only until I get some overtime people in," Tucker announced to the people left at the monitors. Then he gestured for Chase to precede him into the hall and closed the door behind them.

"You just fired four people?"

"Yeah. I did."

"You wanna explain why, cuz?"

"Not really, because even if I do I'm not sure you'll get it through that thick head of yours."

Chase bristled. "What the hell?"

Tucker brushed past him and strode down the hall, turned a corner and, at the end of the second hallway, pushed open the door to his office. Chase followed him and shut the door.

"What's going on, Tuck?"

"That little stunt of yours, Chase."

"What little stunt?"

"At Barron House. Ring a bell?"

"There was no stunt." He was confused. Why would Tucker fire employees whose job it was to watch security monitors?

"Savannah got a boatload of disrespect. From an employee and then from your father. What did you do? You ignored her, and merrily sat with your old man and enjoyed your steak."

"So?"

"Jeez, Chase. You truly are clueless when it comes to women. You didn't see Savannah's face. But those jerks in the monitor room damn sure did. And when I walked in, they were laughing and cracking jokes. About. Your. Wife!"

Chase had never seen his easygoing cousin so angry. He opened his mouth to placate Tucker but the man kept going.

"Instead of going after her, you smile and make nice with Cyrus, sit your ass down at his table and proceed to eat hearty."

"Okay?" Chase still wasn't following.

"Savannah was with me when I stopped in at Security to delete that footage. She stood there and listened to them crack jokes about her and your relationship to her. Thirty minutes later, your *wife* took a cab. With a suitcase and her duffel." Tucker must have seen something in Chase's expression because he softened his tone. "You hurt her, Chase, and she was so upset she was trying to access the wrong elevator when I caught up to her. Then she was witness to the idiocy of our security staff before I could escort her to your rooms. Me, Chase. Not you. Not her husband."

"Oh." Tuck was right; he'd totally messed up. "I'll fix it."

"Seriously?"

"Yes, Tucker, seriously. I have to keep her loyal for a year. I'll do what it takes."

Chase left before Tuck could respond. He rode up to his apartment in the private elevator, thinking. He had stepped on his poncho where Savannah was concerned. He'd sleep on it and come up with a plan.

The next morning, Chase discovered that breakfast was boring without Savannah. That should have been his first clue his life was veering off track. He grabbed his phone and texted Tucker.

Where's Sav headed next?

Tuck's reply came a few moments later. You don't know?

Hello, not her travel agent.

His phone rang in lieu of a text. Tucker's gruff voice exploded in his ear. "No, but you *are* supposed to be her husband."

"Ow. Low blow, cuz."

"It was meant to be, Chase."

"So…where's she headed?"

"San Antonio."

"Cool. I like it there. Wanna go?"

He could picture Tucker rolling his eyes as his cousin replied, "No. Someone has to take care of your business."

Laughing, Chase teased back, "That's why I pay you the big bucks."

Three hours later, he was packed, his calendar cleared. Reservations had been made for a suite in a five-star hotel on the Riverwalk, and he was on board the corporate jet winging to South Texas. He figured he had a day and a half before Savannah arrived. He had a lot to do.

Late Sunday night, Savannah had stopped in Kingman, just over the Nevada-Arizona state line. As she drove, it occurred to her that she wouldn't have stall space in San Antonio until Tuesday evening. She could drive easy instead of pushing it. And since money wasn't a problem, she planned to find stables for overnight boarding and a comfortable hotel to sleep in.

Her conscience twinged a little bit at the thought of spending lots of Chase's money, but only a little bit. Chase Barron was a jerk with way too much money. Her truck and trailer were rolling advertisements for Barron Entertainment, so by golly she would stay first-class from now on, just like the other competitors with big sponsors.

She knew a place just outside Kingman where she could stable Red and Cimarron and park her trailer. She pulled into the Best Western Wayfarer's, got her own room and called the stables. Luckily, she arrived before midnight so the owner was awake and had stalls available. She drove there, got the horses settled and fed, unhitched the trailer, and headed back.

Monday's travels got her to El Paso. The sun was just over an hour from setting as she off-loaded the horses and she decided to give them a workout. Rather than dragging out their tack, she tied off the lead line on Cimarron's halter to use as reins and swung up onto him bareback. The paint pranced sideways, testing her seat. She squeezed with her knees and the horse settled. With Red on a halter rope, she rode out into the field behind the barn.

This was what she loved about the life she'd chosen— on the road, a good horse between her legs, the sky above. Her heart should have been light but it wasn't. Try as she might, she hadn't been able to put aside the hurt from the scene Sunday night. And Chase hadn't bothered to call. Or text.

She rubbed at her left ring finger and noted there was a small rash within the dark circle left by the ring. She needed to get some clear fingernail polish to coat the ring. She'd heard somewhere that it helped seal cheap metal. Her mood shattered now, she rode back to the barn, dismounted and rubbed down both horses. She tossed in a block of hay, poured a measure of grain and made sure they had fresh water.

After a solitary dinner at a Mexican restaurant down the street from the Holiday Inn, Savannah showered, flopped onto the bed with the TV remote and resisted the urge to call Tucker. Doing so was a really bad idea. Tucker had been nice to her, but not only was he Chase's family, he was Chase's second in command. Putting him in the middle of things was way more high school than she was comfortable with.

She found an action-adventure movie starring a hunky actor and settled in to watch. She fell asleep somewhere between a big explosion and the steamy kiss between the star and the beautiful girl he rescued. Savvie didn't turn off the TV and she blamed that fact for the sexy dreams she had, the images leaving her hot, achy and frustrated when she woke up, despite a cold shower, followed by a hot shower. She found herself squirming a lot on her drive to San Antonio.

As she queued up in traffic to turn into San Antonio's AT&T Center, Savannah was rocking out to Luke Bryan's "That's My Kind of Night." In fact, she was singing along and bouncing in her seat so hard she didn't notice the knot of people who surged forward as she pulled up to the horse check-in station. She grabbed her purse and the folder with the horses' veterinary health certificates, put on her Stetson, hopped out of the truck and froze.

Chase recognized the truck and trailer as it idled in line. He'd been hanging around since Monday afternoon and when Savannah hadn't shown up, he'd… *panicked* was too strong a word. He'd been concerned, and as a result, he had Cash's security company locate her by the GPS installed in the truck. When he realized she was taking her time, he was relieved. This gave him more time to set up for her arrival.

And set up he did. He'd already secured her two stalls, feed and hay. He also started the rumor in social media that he and his bride were using her rodeo appearances as an extended honeymoon. The paparazzi were salivating. Any picture of him was a guaranteed paycheck for the freelancers.

Watching as the truck inched closer, Chase felt unaccustomed anticipation build in his gut. Nothing so wimpy as butterflies; the sensation was more like F-16 fighter jets dive-bombing. Though disconcerting, it was still fun—like what Christmas used to be when his mother had been alive. Savannah was doing something inside the cab: bouncing around, waving her arms. He wondered if she was singing along to the radio. That was kinda cute.

As soon as she stopped and climbed out, he headed in her direction. He didn't let the look on her face deter him as he shoved up in her space, took her in his arms and kissed her hard enough to knock her hat off.

Chase eased back on the kiss and whispered against her lips, "Smile, kitten, we're on *Candid Camera*." Then he claimed her lips again and kissed her like a starving man—or a man still celebrating his honeymoon.

Her fists balled against his chest. Was she pushing him away or resisting an urge to grab his shirt and pull him closer? He couldn't decide. He prolonged the kiss for several more long moments before easing back, letting her catch a breath. He stepped to Savannah's side as a rodeo official appeared. The woman wore a huge grin and pantomimed fanning her face.

"Sugar, I gotta admire your tenacity t'hit the circuit, but dang. If that man was my husband, I don't think I'd get out of bed for a year."

"Yeah, easy for you to say," Savannah muttered under her breath, but loud enough for Chase to hear.

Laughing, he hooked his arm around her neck. "That's why I'm here. We might be newlyweds but I love that my woman wants to do things her way, wants to make her mark in her chosen career. I'm proud of Savannah, and I plan on being at the Thomas and Mack

Center in Vegas come December. I'll be cheering when she wins the championship."

He didn't miss the crowd snapping pictures with their cell phones and cameras. He planned to tie her up tight in his web so she was stuck with him, just like their agreement stipulated. Chase had a plan.

Fifteen

Chase didn't give Savannah a chance to protest. He rushed her through check-in, off-loading and feeding the horses. Then he locked up her truck and trailer, herded her to the Ford Explorer he'd leased for the week and swept her off to their five-star suite on the Riverwalk. He had kept the location secret, though that was always subject to change. It all depended on Savannah.

"I thought we'd go out to dinner," he suggested after she'd showered and shed the funky horse-sweat smell.

"Feel free to go without me."

"Kitten." He put a whole heap of *pretty please* and *don't be mad* in that word.

"Don't. Just…don't."

He choked back a laugh. Her lip curled and her nose scrunched as she glowered at him.

"Kitten." This time, his amusement leaked through, along with a dribble of *I think you're cute.*

"No. Won't work. Just…go out to eat. And don't come back. Better yet. You stay in, I'll go out and get a room in another hotel."

"Sweetheart, I'll bet a week's salary that the lobby is swarming with media."

"Then why are you suggesting we go out to eat?"

"Because we can go out the back way, catch a river taxi, have a great dinner and talk."

She crossed her arms, and Chase reminded himself to breathe so he didn't hyperventilate. He loved her breasts, and when she was standing like that, they were plumped and peeking at him through the V of her shirt. He wanted to cup them, kiss them—wanted to kiss her in lots of places, actually. Maybe room service wasn't such a bad idea. He shifted the fly of his jeans and didn't hide the motion.

Her skin flushed. He watched the pink tinge climb from her chest to her neck before it flooded her cheeks. Getting her to blush was almost as much fun as making her mad.

"Fine. We'll go out. What's the dress code? I wouldn't want my lack of taste and sense of propriety to reflect badly on you and your father." She spit the words out, hissing like the wildcat he often compared her to.

He was even more turned on. "There's a Mexican café down on the river. I think you'll like it. And you're dressed fine. Put your boots on and grab a jacket. It's chilly at night on the water."

He waited while she rooted for clean socks, sat on the bed to pull them on and shoved her feet into a pair of boots. She grabbed the fringed leather jacket from the closet and shrugged into it. Then she stood there, thumbs hooked in her front pockets, glare on her face, her breasts still peeking at him from the V of her shirt. He contemplated how angry makeup sex was always fun.

With a shake of her head, she marched across the suite to the door. "Whatever you're thinking, hoss, ain't gonna happen."

He perked up at that slip. *Hoss.* That was infinitely better than many of the names she'd probably tagged him with in the past few days. "After you."

Thirty minutes and a leisurely water taxi ride later, they were seated on the patio of Cantina Cactus. He ordered her a top-shelf margarita on the rocks with extra salt, and a Corona for himself. When the waitress returned with their drinks, Savannah ordered dinner in a clipped voice, ignoring him. He added his order, then leaned back in his chair. He'd debated their seating arrangement and opted to sit across from her.

There were several reasons—he could see her face, and she was basically cornered by the railing surrounding the patio at her back. Mainly, though, she wouldn't be able to see anything he might do beneath the table, like logging into his fake Twitter account and tweet using the #FindChase hashtag. He'd resorted to the ruse to both avoid the paparazzi and to use them as needed. He hoped he didn't have to employ such antics tonight but… One look at Savannah's face, he figured his thumbs would be getting a workout.

After their meal arrived, Savannah rolled a flour tortilla and waved it. "Are you sure you want to do this in public?"

"Do what, kitten?"

"Don't call me that."

"Kitten."

She threw up her hands, still clutching the tortilla. "Gah! What do you want, Chase?"

He composed his expression to what one ex-girlfriend called his dreamy-eyes-and-dimple face. Something flickered in Savannah's eyes so he hoped it was working. "I want you, sweetheart."

"No, you don't."

"Okay, look. I screwed up."

"Ya think?"

"Yes, I think. Which I wasn't doing at the time. Look, darlin', things get intense with my dad. There's a long history there, and I didn't mean for you to get caught in the middle."

"Yes, you did."

Her voice was so soft he wasn't sure he heard her. "Excuse me?"

She raised her chin, and he admired the stubborn tilt. "Yes, you did. You dragged me into the middle the moment you put this ring on my finger." She held up her left hand, fingers splayed.

"I was up front, Savannah."

"So was I. And I made a mistake."

Chase stiffened. If she called off the marriage, he was up a creek full of excrement. "A mistake." He enunciated those words very carefully and there was no question mark at the end when he said them.

"Hands off. I didn't stick to my rule. That was my mistake. I slept with you. I won't be that stupid again."

"Excuse me? Sleeping with me was a mistake? Really? And how many times did you get off?"

Pink colored her cheeks, and she broke eye contact. He'd flustered her. That was good, and his anger receded a little. He couldn't lose control. Not if he wanted her back in his bed—and not just to sleep. Reaching across the table, he clasped her hand, tightening his grip slightly when she tried to pull away.

"Kitten, listen to me. Saturday night was *not* a mistake. Not for me. Yes, twenty-four hours later I totally screwed up. This whole marriage gig is new to me. I'm not used to looking out for someone else. I'll make it up to you."

Savannah raised her eyes to gaze into his. "Don't do this. Don't be nice and apologetic. I don't want to like you. I just want to get through the next twelve months."

"Is everything okay with your food?" The waitress appeared with a water pitcher.

Chase glanced up at her. "Everything is fine, thanks." After the woman wandered off, he realized the moment had passed. He'd have to activate Operation Twitter. "Eat up, kitten, before your dinner gets cold."

Following his own advice, he shoveled several bites of his chiles rellenos into his mouth. After a sip of his beer, he dropped his hands to his lap and started typing. Time to pull in the big guns.

Savannah stood on the balcony of their suite watching the traffic on the Riverwalk. Water taxis cruised, leaving gentle waves in their wake. Pedestrians thronged and a mix of music floated up.

She'd managed to choke down only half her tamales before the paparazzi found them. She'd had to pose with Chase, a smile on her face, and then eyes closed in pretended bliss while he kissed her—his way of bribing them to go away. They didn't go far, and the restaurant staff sneaked the newlyweds out through the kitchen.

Savannah's feelings were all over the map where Chase was concerned. She didn't trust him. Couldn't trust him for so many reasons.

He was a player. Egotistical. Self-centered enough to be a narcissist. Yet when he smiled—the smile that played peekaboo with his dimple and lit up his eyes— she could fall in love with Chase Barron. Way too easily. And if she did, he'd only break her heart. She was a means to an end. A convenient wife in inconvenient circumstances.

"Kitten?"

She hadn't heard the door behind her open but Chase was suddenly there, his arm circling her waist and pulling her to him. The hard length of him nestled against her bottom. She didn't realize how chilly she'd been until his heat surrounded her.

"You should go to bed," she said briskly.

"As soon as you come with me."

"I'm sleeping on the couch."

"Savannah." He swept her hair off her neck before his lips began to nibble. She stiffened, but he just held her tighter. "I said I was sorry, Sav. I meant it. But we're still married. We're still good together in bed. Why deny ourselves that pleasure?"

"It's a bad idea, Chase."

"No, it's not. In fact, I want you to see a doctor tomorrow."

Her head jerked up and connected with his face.

"Ow. Damn, woman. You tryin' to kill me?"

She twisted and turned but now he had her back

braced against the railing. She hadn't bloodied his nose, thankfully, but she was still wary. "Why do I have to see a doctor?"

"Birth control. I'm clean. You said you hadn't dated in a long time—"

Heat suffused her face, and she pushed against his chest with her palms. "I don't want to talk about this."

"Sav, it's okay. I figure you're clean, too. I'm always careful, but with you? With you, I want it all. I want to feel you surrounding me, with no barrier between us. That's all I'm sayin'. Okay?"

Her agreement came out a little breathier than she would have preferred. This man got to her—in all the wrong ways. She didn't—couldn't—fight when he dipped his head and his mouth sought out hers. His tongue teased, asking for entrance, and she parted her lips even as she parted her legs so he could stand between them, his hot, hard desire evident as he rubbed against her center.

"Come to bed, Savannah," he murmured against her cheek when he broke the kiss. He backed away just enough to sweep her into his arms.

He carried her inside to the bedroom and settled her on the bed. "Be right back," he whispered. She heard him out in the living area shutting and locking the balcony door, closing drapes, checking the security bar on the front door. Then he was back, shedding clothes as he approached her.

"Seeing you lying there, it's like Christmas. I get to unwrap you and find the present beneath."

Her heart melted even as her brain jumped up and down trying to get her attention. She ignored the logic and went for emotion. Tonight—*just* tonight—she'd take what he had to offer. He'd make her feel cherished and wanted. He'd soothe her loneliness with gentle but demanding hands. He'd make love to her, even if it was only sex in his mind. She could live with that. Yes, for a year, she'd take what he offered. And when the time came, she'd walk away and hope her heart survived.

Sixteen

That week in San Antonio passed like a dream. Savannah's times remained top-notch, and while Chase didn't hover, he was around. A lot. He hung out in the contestants' hospitality room. He took her to dinner. They held hands. He made her laugh. And his kisses curled her toes despite her best intentions. He made love to her at night in ways sweet and sometimes dirty, but always satisfying.

She'd broached the subject of his work, but he waved away her concerns. "I can work anywhere I have a laptop, sweetheart."

And it seemed that he could.

Then it was Sunday. She won the barrel racing and picked up her check from the rodeo office, but even more importantly, she added points to her total. Chase was in the mood to celebrate, so they did. They went to New Braunfels, ate, and then partied and danced at Gruene Hall to a live band. Savvie never considered herself much of a dancer but Chase could boot scoot with the best of them.

They returned to the hotel, ordered up late-night appetizers, fed each other, drank beer, laughed and fell into bed happy. Chase made love to her slow and easy, much like their night had been, and she fell a little more in love with him.

He followed her to Bakersfield, Beaumont, Wichita. To Helena, Minot, Abilene. She participated in a few all-girl rodeos along the way but Chase didn't stray. She didn't hide her face in checkout lines because they'd faded from the tabloids. Paparazzi occasionally popped up, but there was nothing juicy about an apparently happily married billionaire and his cowgirl bride.

Savannah relaxed. And that was her first mistake. They'd been together for almost six months. Chase was off in the Bahamas wheeling and dealing over some big new resort. She'd been on her own for a week and was settled in her hotel in Reno, gearing up for the weekend and the rodeo. While the hotel wasn't a Barron property, it was luxurious, and she was treated like a VIP. Like so many of the big hotels in Reno, it had a casino and restaurants. After her experience in Vegas, she shied away from those. She wanted a comfortable place where a cowgirl could sit and eat a burger, drink a beer and maybe listen to some county music on a jukebox.

The hotel doorman directed her to Riley's Saloon and got a cab for her. "Hard to park, and if you have more than a beer or two, you'll want to take a cab back. Local cops have a no-tolerance rule."

She'd learned to tip doormen and cabdrivers. Hers passed over his card, told her to call when she was ready to go back to the hotel and tipped his baseball cap to her. She walked into Riley's to the sounds of Toby Keith's "I Love This Bar." Perfect.

After her eyes adjusted to the lower lights, she looked around. There were a few tourist types, but it was mostly locals and several tables of rodeo cowboys. A couple of the guys nodded or waved, and one stood up. He motioned her over to the empty chair at his table. Jess Lyon was a cowboy's cowboy and a cowgirl's dream come true—ruggedly handsome, broad shouldered, a hint of bad boy in his grin. Savannah had known him forever.

Full from her burger, mellow after two beers and comfortable in her surroundings, she leaned back in her chair. Jess's arm was draped across the top and her shoulders brushed against it. Carrie Underwood was singing about taking a smoke break, and Jess leaned in to speak directly into Savvie's ear.

"Heard a rumor, sugar."

"Oh?"

"Yup. Seems someone's photo just got added to the NFR site under barrel racing's leaders."

She squealed and, without thinking, turned in her chair, grabbed his face and laid a smacking kiss on his lips. Then she grabbed her phone from her hip pocket and started Googling the National Finals Rodeo site. There she was. She was hot on the trail of the top leaders. She thumbed over to her contacts list and hit Chase's number, all prepared to give him the good news.

Her call rolled to voice mail. Disappointed, she left

a message amid shouted congratulations from the cowboys in the bar. Celebrating, she stayed later than she'd planned, drank more beer than she should have and ended up accepting a ride back to her hotel with Jess. He left her at the front entrance in the doorman's solicitous hands, driving away to her shouted thanks.

Reno was another conquest. She walked away with a first place and a hefty check. Her life was good and next up was Cheyenne Frontier Days. Chase had promised to meet her there. While she hated to admit it, she missed him—and not just in her bed. She missed his boyish grin and the mischievous twinkle in his eyes. She missed holding his hand as they walked and the sound of his voice. She'd called him several times—getting voice mail—but she left messages telling him that she missed him and was looking forward to reconnecting in Cheyenne.

Tucker had leased a condo for them in Cheyenne and made arrangements to board Red and Cimarron at a nearby ranch. She had a week off and once Chase arrived, she planned on taking some vacation time with him.

After arriving in Cheyenne and settling in, Savannah went to the grocery store to stock up and was pushing her basket toward the cashier when one of the tabloids caught her eye.

She sucked in a sharp breath, then lost it in a whoosh as she caught the two pictures on the cover. One was of Chase, standing with a model-thin woman in a backless dress. Chase, with his hand resting on the small of her naked back. Chase, smiling his sexy grin into the lens of the camera. The other photo featured Savannah. In Riley's, kissing Jess.

Oh, no. Nonononono. This was bad. Very, very bad! She didn't hesitate. She grabbed all the copies and dumped them into her basket. She checked out, numb to everything around her. Getting the grocery bags to her pickup was a struggle. Getting in her truck was harder. Driving while panic blurred her vision was almost impossible.

Finally back at the condo, she dragged her purchases inside and left them on the kitchen counter. She called Chase. Voice mail. Again. She managed to leave a choked "Call me, please!" before she cut the call and dialed Tucker. Voice mail. She left the same message. How could things go so wrong?

Chase ignored his phone and glared when Tucker's rang. Wisely, his cousin didn't answer, either. He shoved the tabloid across the coffee table. "Wanna explain this?"

Tucker glanced down, then met his gaze. "Not me who was out with Diane Brandenburg."

"I wasn't out with her. And I damn sure didn't kiss her."

"Jealous?"

"Of what?"

"The fact your wife was kissing another man."

"Wife in name only, cuz, as she's proved."

"You claim being with Di was innocent. Has it occurred to you that Savannah is innocent?"

"I didn't kiss Di."

"And Savannah was in a bar, sitting at a table with eight other people. Savvie is not the type to make out in front of an audience."

"How do you know?"

Tucker stared at him, his expression incredulous.

"This *is* Savannah we're talking about, Chase. Not even Cash could turn up dirt on her. She's had a couple of semiserious boyfriends—one in high school, one in college." His cousin studied him for several long moments. "You really like this girl."

"No, I don't," Chase answered quickly. From the arched brow he got in return, maybe too quickly. "It's business, Tucker. Always has been." He muttered a few cusswords under his breath.

"Ah, so all that spending time with her, holding hands, kissing for the cameras was just…work."

"No, it was to make a point to my father. And the minute I was out of sight, she didn't bother to stay in touch." His phone pinged again. Irritated, he jerked it out of his pocket and scrolled to Voice. He had over thirty messages. All from the same number. Savannah's. "What the hell?"

He checked the times and dates. The calls went all the way back to the week she was in Reno, including the night she was in that bar with that cowboy Casanova. Well, this would be good. He hit Playback and put it on speaker.

"Chase! Chase! Guess what! Jess just gave me the news. I made the NFR leaderboard. I'm on the website. So excited. Everyone here is thrilled. Me, too. Miss you. Call me when you get this! Bye!"

He refused to meet Tucker's disapproving gaze as they listened to the next message. "Hey, baby. A little drunk but I'm back at the hotel. Jess gave me a ride. He'd like to meet you 'cause he says you make me happy. You do, you know." She giggled. "I shouldn't admit that. Miss you, hoss. Bunches."

They listened to each voice mail she'd left, ending

with her final two, the choked "Call me, please," left several minutes before. It was the first call he'd deliberately ignored. The last message was a soft sob and a whispered "I'm sorry."

"Yeah, that definitely sounds like a woman playing you for a fool, Chase."

"Shut up, Tucker. Why the hell didn't I get these calls when she made them?"

"Good question. I'll try to find out."

Two hours later, Chase landed at the Cheyenne Airport and drove directly to the resort where Tucker had leased the condo. Savannah's truck was parked in front of one of the rustic redwood buildings. He didn't bother stopping at the office to grab a key. If Savannah wouldn't let him in, he'd kick in the door and pay for the damages.

He parked his rental SUV, left his bag in the vehicle and marched up to the door. It was jerked open as he raised his hand to knock. Savannah's eyes were red rimmed and puffy. She'd been crying. Her expression shifted from hopeful to guarded then back. He did the only thing he could think of under the circumstances. He opened his arms, and she fell into them.

"I'm so sorry, Chase. So-o-o sorry. I didn't know a reporter was there. It was just some of the rodeo crew."

"Shh, kitten, s'okay."

"Nonono. I kissed Jess. I did. But it didn't mean anything. I was just excited when I got the news. He's a friend. Just a friend. He was there. I was excited so I grabbed him. That's all. He has a fiancée. I promise. Just a friend."

"Savannah." He moved her inside and got the door

shut behind them. "Easy, honey. Deep breaths. And please don't cry." He managed to get her to the couch and settled in his lap before her breathing was under control. In normal circumstances—with any other woman—tears had no effect on him. Savannah's tears ripped into his heart with sharp kitten claws. He didn't want to make her cry. Not ever.

"I called," she hiccuped. "That night. You didn't answer. I kept calling."

"Glitch in the system. I didn't know you'd called, sweetheart. None of the times. And I was busy and didn't think to call you." He kissed her forehead. "Congrats on making the top twenty, kitten. Sorry I wasn't there to celebrate with you."

She sniffled and wiped her nose with her sleeve before taking a very deep breath. Twisting her head, she glanced at the pile of glossy papers on the coffee table. "What's going to happen?"

"Nothing. Tucker is doing damage control in the media, and I've already discussed the situation with my family."

"Uh-huh." She stiffened slightly. "I… Who…"

"She's a model, Sav. Diane Brandenburg. She was there on the island for a photo shoot. We weren't *together* together. Just casually at that cocktail party."

"Promise?"

"Promise." He didn't hesitate to answer, even though he'd considered inviting Di back to his room. Doing so would have created more trouble than any pleasure he might have gotten. That was what he'd told himself, anyway, because the alternative—that he wanted to be only with Savannah—was too big to contemplate. While Di was all sleek and built for fast sex, Savannah was curvy and comfortable. Running his hand along her side and hip, stroking down her thigh and back up, was soothing. And sweet. And felt like home.

Seventeen

Savannah awoke tangled in the blankets. After making love—several times—she and Chase had fallen into exhausted sleep, bodies pressed together, legs entwined, her head on his chest. From the position she found herself in upon opening her eyes, she figured neither of them had moved.

"Mornin', kitten."

"Howdy, hoss." She smiled against his warm skin. "Want some coffee?"

"Can you make it from here?"

"Don't think so."

"Damn. You gonna let me kiss you before I brush my teeth?"

A giggle escaped her and her shoulders shook with repressed laughter. "Maybe your morning breath cancels out mine."

"Let's find out."

Chase tightened his arms around her back and urged her higher in the bed. His mouth found hers and he kissed her deeply. He tasted of sex and chocolate mints and she wondered if she could find a coffee flavor to match because that would be heaven to wake up to every morning. Not that she was addicted to coffee. Or to Chase.

He broke the kiss but didn't let go. In fact, he nibbled along her jawline until he reached her ear. He sucked her lobe in before kissing the soft spot behind it. Then he trailed down her neck, along the crest of her shoulder before dipping to her breast, which had her moaning in the back of her throat and arching into him.

"Want you, kitten."

He didn't give her a chance to answer as he rolled her onto her back. While he laved her breasts, his hand smoothed down her belly and cupped her. "Spread, darlin'."

She shifted her legs and his fingers dipped into her heat. Arching her hips, she sought his touch. Shivering in anticipation, she concentrated on breathing and absorbing the absolute pleasure of their lovemaking.

"Please," she gasped, wanting him—all of him—inside her.

He obliged, shifting his weight to rest between her legs, teasing her for a moment before sinking in. Their sighs of completion echoing one another, they lay still as if stunned by the enormity of their feelings—both physical and emotional. Then he moved, slowly lifting his hips as he slid out before gliding in deep. She hooked her heels around his waist and hung on as his tempo increased. He might be on top but she could still ride him, and she did. When they tumbled over the edge, they did it together, the circle complete.

The next week passed in similar fashion. They made love upon awakening, sharing coffee and breakfast before another round of sexy times in the shower. Then they braved the outdoors. They went sightseeing. They went horseback riding. Chase discovered he enjoyed the horses. The ranch had always been his home, but he'd never been one for the great outdoors and all the activities that went on there. Cord, Chance and Cash had done the whole hunting, fishing and riding thing. Clay was the scholar and was almost ten years older. While he'd wanted to emulate his oldest brother, Chase didn't hang around Clay much. He'd retreated into books—adventures and tales of derring-do.

Now, atop a horse, surrounded by the Rocky Mountains, and in the company of a beautiful woman, he believed he'd come into his own. Tucker had ridden hard on him, reminding him that if Savvie had to be monogamous during the term of the contract, he should, too. He didn't want to admit that he had no desire to stray.

As they rode into a mountain meadow, Chase and Savvie startled a herd of elk. Reining their mounts to a stop, they watched as a magnificent bull elk threw back his head and trumpeted a challenge at their intrusion. Chase laughed, understanding the animal's territorial stand. He'd felt the same when he first saw the picture of Savannah kissing that cowboy.

They skirted the meadow, found another trail and followed it, leaving the bull behind to protect his cows. A sense of contentment stole over Chase, and he urged

Red closer to Cimarron so he could reach over and snag Savannah's hand.

"This is nice."

Her concerned expression softened as she smiled at him. "It is. Not sure I could live up here. It's beautiful but…" She glanced around, then up, taking in the towering peaks. "I guess I'm an Oklahoma girl born and bred. The biggest mountains I want to spend time in are the Wichitas or the Arbuckles. I *like* the wide-open spaces."

He squeezed her hand in agreement. "I've turned into a city boy, and I don't go home much. Maybe I should. My granddad used to say that once you got red dirt on your hands, it soaked in and got in your blood, became such a part of you that you'd never be happy away from it."

"Are you happy?"

"What do you mean?"

"Living in Las Vegas. Traveling like you do. I mean to Hollywood. Nashville. All those exotic places you go."

They rode in silence as he contemplated her question. "I was. I love what I do, Savannah. Barron Entertainment is my red dirt. I'm good at running hotels, picking places to put them and watching them get built. I like dabbling in the true entertainment side—movies, and the new record company. Radio and TV. All of it."

"Is this okay?"

He didn't like the hesitation in her voice. "Is what okay?"

"This." He still held her right hand so she dropped the reins in her left and used it to wave between them.

"Us. You spending this time here with me instead of doing work stuff."

Something warm spread through his chest. She was worried about him. He liked that. "Yes, kitten. This is very okay. Tuck is my second in command. He can deal with most situations. I've picked good people to work for me. And truthfully?" He leaned closer to make sure she was gazing into his eyes when he spoke again. "There's no place I'd rather be."

That was the truth. He didn't just feel content, he felt complete when he was with Savannah. Was he falling in love with her? Was that a good thing or bad? How did she feel about him? He studied the expressions flickering across her face. He liked the one that settled in place.

"I think that's the nicest thing anyone's ever said to me." She squeezed his hand and murmured something that made his breath catch. He wasn't positive, but it sounded like she'd added that she was falling in love with him. He inhaled, relaxed, tugged the hand he held to his mouth and kissed the back of it.

Happy, they rode in silence, turning by mutual agreement back toward the stables. This was the last day of their alone time. The rodeo started tomorrow, and Savannah would be focused on her events. Chase had several deals in the works and really needed to spend some time going over paperwork and discussing things with his staff. He'd fit that in around watching Savannah compete. Something else he'd learned—he enjoyed the heck out of watching his wife do her thing. He'd had to pull some major strings to get tickets in a box where he could see all the action. Instructing Tucker to add a line item to the budget to

become a major sponsor of next year's Frontier Days
would take care of that situation.

Two days later, the rodeo was in full swing. Savannah was in her element and having a blast. As good
as her rodeo run was, her personal life was even better. The absolute craziest thing had happened. She'd
fallen in love with a Barron—the biggest playboy in
the Barron barn, in fact. And while she didn't have
much experience or a great track record with the men
she had dated, she'd almost bet that Chase felt the same
about her. He didn't say the words but there was something about the way he looked at her, especially when
he thought she wasn't paying attention, the way he
touched her, the way he made love to her at night. Despite her best intentions, Chase had captured her heart.

He'd sent her a text right before her first run of the
day wishing her luck and complaining that business
had come up that he needed to take care of. He apol-
ogized for missing her competition and promised to
contact her as soon as he knew what was going on.
She'd received a second text a couple hours later asking her to meet him for dinner before the rodeo concert that night. Chase's cousin Deacon Tate and his
Sons of Nashville band were the featured performers
and Chase had gotten them fantastic seats. It always
helped to have family connections.

She'd had a great day, once again coming out on top
in the barrel racing. She was quickly working her way
up the ranks of the top twenty riders on the Wrangler
National Finals Rodeo list.

Now, showered, primped—she'd put on a filmy
skirt and blouse—and ready for some fun, she was

all but floating when she walked into the restaurant. The hostess beamed a huge smile her direction as she approached.

"Hi. I'm meeting—"

"Mr. Barron, right?" The girl cut her off. "He's waiting for you in the lounge."

"Oh! Thanks." She returned the smile and headed in the direction the hostess pointed.

The bar was separate from the dining area, down a hallway decorated with Western art. Savannah could hear music, the clink of glasses and the clack of balls on a pool table. She stepped through the door and glanced around. The place was a fusion of roadhouse bar and upscale cocktail lounge. It shouldn't have worked but it did.

The corners were shadowy, the tables and booths lit by candles in old-fashioned lanterns. She scanned the area, looking for Chase. He wasn't sitting at any of the tables, and she was about to walk through and check each of the booths when two men standing at the bar moved aside. She caught sight of Chase's profile and headed toward him. She was halfway there when the whole scene coalesced in her brain.

He wasn't alone. A woman stood with him. Against him, actually, pressed between his spread thighs as he sat on a leather-seated bar stool. Her hands rested on his shoulders, and she was smiling. She wore a form-fitting dress with no back, and Chase's hand rested on her bare skin, his fingers inside the draped material.

The woman turned and looked right through Savannah, who recognized her. It was the model photographed with Chase in the Bahamas. Frozen to the spot, Savvie didn't know what to do. She couldn't breathe, couldn't move, could only watch as the beautiful model leaned closer and kissed Chase, as Chase tightened his arm around her back, his whole hand disappearing inside her dress. As he looked right at Savannah while he kissed Diane Brandenburg, his expression one of smug conceit.

Tears burned her eyes, muting the scene with blurry watercolors. Too bad she couldn't dull the sharp pain in her chest, the sense of betrayal. She watched Chase move his head, whisper something to the model. Savvie stood there while the woman tossed her perfect blond hair over her shoulder so she could see Savannah. She saw that pair of eyes, so brilliantly blue she could tell the color in the half-light. She heard the low, throaty laugh that was both sexy and dismissive.

Chase didn't move when the woman nibbled on his ear and whispered something back. He just watched, one corner of his mouth quirked. Sardonic. That was another word her English professor had used that Savannah had never known the true meaning of. Not until that moment.

The music from the jukebox stopped playing as the moment stretched out. Her phone rang. She ignored it, her brain still incapable of controlling her muscles. The woman moved, turning in Chase's embrace. She slid an arm around his neck and cocked her hip to press against his groin. Her lips were curled in a cat-ate-the-canary smile that didn't reach the ice blue of her eyes. A part of Savannah's brain wondered how a woman could betray another woman like this. Then she understood. She was the interloper here. She was the one who didn't belong.

The room had grown silent and nobody moved, as

though the moment had been frozen in time, a photograph capturing a momentous occasion. Heart breaking, Savannah inhaled. She would not cry. She'd already shed too many tears over this man. No more. Straightening her shoulders and raising her chin, she pasted a proud smile on her face—a smile that cost her everything to manufacture and hold in place. All she had left was her dignity. She refused to give Chase the satisfaction of seeing her fall apart.

She turned her back. Placed one foot in front of the other until she was out of the room. Until she was down the hallway and past all those people lined up to eat and laugh and have a good time. Until she was outside under the summer sky. Until she was safely inside her truck. Driving. Then inside the condo. Staring at the bed where she and Chase had made love less than twelve hours ago.

Savannah wouldn't sleep in that bed. What if he'd brought that woman here? Had sex with her in that bed. She couldn't bear it if she buried her face in the pillow she'd slept on last night and smelled someone else's perfume. Her phone rang again.

This time her fingers worked and she retrieved it from her purse. It was Tucker. She should have turned the phone off but she didn't. Obviously a glutton for punishment, she answered.

"Savvie, hi. I've been trying to reach you. Chase is stuck here in Vegas and still in the emergency meeting. He asked me to step out and call you."

She didn't say anything so he continued. "He's sorry about missing Deke's concert but says you should go without him. Deke wants to meet you and will be watching for you."

She still didn't speak.

"Sav? Are you there?"

"I can't believe he's got you doing his dirty work, Tucker."

His voice turned cautious as he asked, "Sugar? Is everything all right? What's going on?"

"I know what his business is, Tucker. I just saw him with that model. Di whatever-her-name-is. Tell him nice try, but I won't be falling for his lies anymore. Tell him not to bother coming back here. I'll keep my end of the bargain so long as he doesn't contact me again."

Savannah dropped the phone from her ear and tapped the end call button. Then she turned off her phone. No longer hungry, she wanted only to get numb. The ache in her chest made it hard to breathe. She wanted to get mad at Chase, but how could she be angry at him? She knew who and what he was. She should be furious with herself. *She* had let her guard down. *She* had let him worm his way into her bed and her heart. This was all her fault. She knew better but she did it, anyway.

"You, Savannah Wolfe, are an absolute, complete idiot." Announcing it to the empty room didn't help. There was a six-pack of beer in the fridge. Maybe if she drank all of them, she could take the edge off the pain. She and alcohol weren't exactly friends, but maybe if she killed off enough bottles, she would stop missing him. Maybe fall asleep. Without dreams. Because dreams just messed up everything.

Eighteen

Chase was desperate to get back to Cheyenne. He had no idea what Savannah thought she'd seen, but he had to get to her, talk to her, fix things. Tucker had talked to her at 7:30 p.m. It was now 2:00 a.m. and the plane was still twenty minutes from landing. He'd tried calling her cell and left so many voice mails that the last time he called, the message said her mailbox was full. He called the condo phone. It just rang.

He'd been stuck in a meeting of other casino managers, the Clark County district attorney, and a police task force that included the FBI, US Marshals Service and lawyers from the Justice Department to discuss a fraud ring working the casino. He'd walked out during a break, informing the authorities there was an emergency with his wife. Luckily, no one had tried to stop him, otherwise he'd be in jail for assaulting a federal officer.

Just after 3:00 a.m., he was pounding up the walkway to the condo's front door. Savannah's truck was parked in its spot. That was a plus. He put his key in the door. The first lock clicked and he pushed. Nothing budged. She'd thrown the dead bolt. Fine. His key fit both locks. In moments, he was inside.

The TV flickered on some infomercial and Savannah was curled up on the couch, huddled under a throw blanket. Why wasn't she in bed? Gazing down at her, he noticed her thick eyelashes were matted and the skin around her eyes puffy. She'd been crying. Even in sleep her breath hitched. Kneeling beside her, he carefully moved her hair off her face so he could see her better in the low light.

Savannah erupted off the couch, pushing and shoving, reminding him of the first time they'd met. He gathered her close before she could get any momentum, and with a quick twist, settled on the couch with her in his lap, her legs trapped by one of his, her arms encircled by his. She squirmed and fought.

"Shh, kitten. Shh."

"Get out." She didn't scream, which might have been better. Instead, her voice carried the cold disdain of a dead relationship.

"No."

"Then I'll leave. Let me go."

"No. You aren't going anywhere until we settle this."

"Settle this? Settle what? I saw you, Chase. I saw you tonight in that bar with that woman. Kissing her."

"Whoa, whoa, whoa. What bar and what woman? Honey, I flew to Vegas yesterday. I texted you."

"Oh, yeah. You texted. Told me you had some work

and you'd be back in touch. You definitely did that. What I want to know is why. I never pegged you as being cruel."

He breathed deliberately to keep his temper in check. First, he had to get to the bottom of things. Then he'd go pound on someone. "I'd never hurt you, kitten."

"Don't. Call. Me. That." She hissed and snarled, renewing her efforts to get free. He was truly glad she worked with her hands so her nails were short and rounded. Harder to claw his eyes out that way.

"Savannah. I can't fix what's wrong if you don't talk to me."

"Fix what's wrong? You can't fix this. You leave my bed—our bed—lie to me, meet that bimbo, then make sure I see you? How is that fixable? Oh! And then you have your cousin call me to make up some excuse. What happened? You texted me instead of her about dinner? Except you didn't seem surprised to see me, and you made damn sure I saw you lay a big, fat wet one on her."

"Dammit, darlin'. Back up. What are you talking about?"

"You texted me, telling me to meet you for dinner before the concert. So I did. Only you were in the bar with that…that skinny skank from the Bahamas. The one you said means nothing to you. Only you were all over her like stink on sh—"

"Savannah! Look at me." He took a chance and cupped her cheek, easing her face around to look at him. "I didn't text you a second time."

"Yeah. Right."

"Honey, I didn't. When I landed at McCarron Airport, my plane was met by the Feds, and I was escorted to the Clark County Courthouse. I spent all day and most of the freaking night with a bunch of attorneys, the FBI and more cops than I ever want to see again. I don't know who you thought you saw—"

"Shut up, Chase. I saw you. You sat there on that bar stool with that model between your legs, your hand in the back of her dress stroking her butt."

"Model?" He searched his memory, hit on a name. "Di Brandenburg?"

"Yeah, her. You said something to her and she turned around to look at me like I was…pond scum or something. Then she whispered in your ear and the two of you kissed. You. Kissed. Her! Looking at me the whole time."

"Aw hell, kitten." A headache bloomed behind his eyes as he rested his head against her shoulder. "I'm going to kill him."

Savannah didn't breathe for a minute. Her voice squeaked when she asked, "Him who?"

"Cash. We're identical twins. Most people can't tell us apart."

She opened her mouth, probably to dispute his assertion, but then snapped it shut. She studied him hard. His hair. Eyes. Nose. Mouth. Then his eyes again. Her gaze stayed there, unblinking, before she closed her eyes and kept them that way for a few minutes.

"Your eyes. Your eyes are different."

No one had ever noted that difference and he was curious what she thought she saw. "How so?"

"Even when you were angry, back when we first met and you threw me out? You weren't…cold. Mad, yes. But there was this look, this…it was…" She shrugged and struggled to find a description.

"It was what?"

"You looked resigned, but there was humor there, like the world is a big joke and you're the only who gets it."

"Okay…" He stretched out the word. "And?"

"And last night…your brother. There's something in his eyes. Hard. He has hard eyes."

"I'm gonna kill him. For real." Chase gazed into her eyes. "I'm sorry, kitten."

"Why would he do that to you?"

"Don't know, but I suspect Dad put him up to it. Whatever the reason, I plan to find out." His gaze dropped to her mouth and he placed a gentle kiss on her lips. "First, though, I want to make love to my wife."

Chase made one phone call to Tucker's brother, Bridger—who was second in command at Cash's security company—and got Cash's location. He seemed surprised when he opened his hotel room door to find Chase standing there. Pushing inside, Chase studied his twin as he shut the door and sauntered across the room to the coffeemaker. He poured a cup without offering one to Chase.

"You're a jackass."

Cash swallowed a sip of coffee while watching him over the rim of the cup, but made no comment. They stared at each for several minutes before Chase broke the silence.

"What the hell, Cash? Why did you set up Savannah like that?"

"It's for your own good."

"My own good? You have no clue what's good for me."

"Then I'm doing it for the good of the family."

Stunned, Chase stared at his brother. It was like looking into a mirror, but seeing only the dark side of their personalities. "Family. Gotcha. So the old man put you up to this."

"Somebody has to look out for you. This woman is an inconvenient complication in your life. She's only after your money."

"Yeah? You're wrong, Cash. Not everyone is like our old man."

"You think I'm wrong? I plan to prove it to you."

"Stay away from Savannah, Cash. This is your only warning."

Chase hated the expression on his twin's face. Ugly, twisted and angry. What had happened to Cash to put that look in his eyes?

"You gonna choose that bimbo over your family?"

"I love her."

He hadn't meant to say the words. Not out loud. And definitely not to Cash or anyone else in his family. Savannah should have had those words first, not the angry man facing him. Chase knew what they all believed. But Savannah wasn't what they thought she was, wasn't *who* they thought she was. She was sweet and funny. Warm. Loyal. Every bit as special as his three sisters-in-law. He knew as soon as those words were out of his mouth they were true. He did love Savannah, and he wanted her in his world far longer than the year they'd agreed to. He wanted her for a lifetime.

"You love her? What the hell do you know about love, Chase? How many women have you bedded, then kicked out to chase the next one? Dad damn sure gave you the right name. This one isn't anything special. She's just one more notch on your bedpost."

"You're wrong. She's the one, Cash. Like Cassidy is for Chance. Like Jolie always was for Cord. Like Georgie and Clay."

"Jeez, Chase. When did you become whipped like them?"

"Jeez, Cash, when did you become such a bastard?"

"We only have one of those in our family."

"Yeah, our old man."

"No, our ranch foreman."

Chase rocked back on his heels. "Wow. You went there. What the hell is going on with you, Cash?"

"Nothing."

"That's bull. You've been on a mission to be a complete jackass since Chance hooked up with Cassidy."

"Someone needs to worry about this family."

"And your way of doing that is to keep all of us single and miserable?" He rubbed his fingers through his hair, leaving it tousled. "I... Dammit, Cash, you seem like a stranger lately. You're my brother. My *twin*, for God's sake."

"You're the one who married a stranger." Cash looked unapologetic and angry, his hands fisted at his sides and his shoulders tensed, as though he wanted to throw a punch.

"She's not a stranger now. Would you be happier if I'd married Janiece? Talk about a gold digger. That woman spends money like it's dirt, and that whole deal was some business thing concocted by Dad. I would never love Janiece."

Chase's cell vibrated in his hip pocket and he pulled it out. Savannah. He very suddenly craved the sound of her voice, the touch of her hand in his. "Someday, Cash. Someday it will happen to you. Someday you'll find the woman you love and I hope to hell you aren't stupid enough to lose her. We're done here. My wife is calling."

He turned on his heel and headed for the door, his phone to his ear. "Howdy, kitten. I'm on my way."

"You okay, hoss?"

He wasn't, but he wouldn't admit that to her. She'd worry even more. "S'all good, darlin'. I'll be there shortly and will meet you behind the chutes. Gotta give my girl a good-luck kiss before she rides."

Silence stretched between them, then he heard her breathe. "Am I? Your girl?"

"Yeah, kitten. You are."

Nineteen

Chase had insisted they go out for brunch and explained his reasons. "Kitten, you can bet there were photos taken last night in the bar. It's just a matter of time before they hit the tabloids. We're going out for breakfast. I'm tweeting our location—"

"Wait! What?"

He blushed all the way to the tips of his ears, a look Savannah found oddly endearing. "I…sort of have a fake Twitter account and hashtag."

"You have a hashtag?" She didn't know whether to laugh or worry about the guy's need for attention.

"Yes. When I want to be seen, I type—" he held up two fingers on each hand and made a hashtag of them "—hashtag FindChase."

Her eyes widened, once she understood the implications. "Wait! You set me up. In San Antonio. And other places."

He had the good grace not to lie. "It worked, didn't it?" He leaned down and kissed her. She meant to break away, until his arms wrapped around her and he deepened the kiss. By the time he finished, she was on her toes, one leg hitched around his hip, her arms clenched around his neck as she held on for dear life.

"Damn, kitten. Keep that up and I'll have you for breakfast."

Laughing, she pushed away and got her bearings. "I'm hungry." As his gaze grew heated, she quickly added, "For food."

"Tweeting comes in handy. Like now. I'll *leak* our location. Somebody will ask about last night. I'll explain it was Cash. Then I'll kiss you."

"Uh-huh. And why will you kiss me?"

"Because I like kissing you?" He offered his boyish grin—the one with a hint of dimple—and a wink. "Technically, it's a photo op. We're still newlyweds in love."

"What if they ask about the skinny skank?"

He choked back a laugh but it erupted as a snort. "That *skank* is one of the world's highest paid models, wildcat."

"So?"

"If the subject comes up, I'll reasonably point out that the photo allegedly showing me with her was actually Cash, and that they're having a secret affair." He waggled his brows and it was her turn to giggle and snort.

"Turnabout is fair play, and payback is hell."

"My thinking exactly."

Brunch had played out as expected and then he'd kissed her goodbye, sending her off to the rodeo grounds. Unable to leave well enough alone, she'd called him. She had to make sure he was okay. His brother had cut him to the quick. The experience—and profound sense of betrayal—left her feeling shaky, too. She wanted assurances from Chase, wanted him to understand why she needed them.

She was riding Cimarron, warming him up in the practice arena, when she noticed Chase standing at the gate. She slowed the horse's canter to a trot, then a walk as she approached. He opened the gate and she rode through before stopping and dismounting.

"Howdy, kitten." Chase's voice held a hint of something sad.

"Howdy, hoss. You got a kiss for me?"

"Always, baby." He dipped his head and brushed his lips across hers.

Need blossomed within her. And desire. This man had worked his way under her skin in a way no other had. By mutual consent, they started walking, Cimarron trailing along as she led him by the reins.

"How bad was it?"

Chase's expression firmed, the skin around his eyes tightening. "About like I expected."

She slipped her hand into his and he laced their fingers. "I'm sorry, Chase."

"No, I'm sorry. I saw your face last night. I…" He cleared his throat. "I've been a lot of things in my life. I've done a lot I'm not proud of." Hesitating, he tugged her to a stop. "I wouldn't set you up like that, Savannah. If I was going to step out on you, I'd be honest and tell you."

Her chest grew tight, and she worked to keep her expression bland, obviously failing as his eyes softened. "I'd tell you, and I wouldn't do it in public. It's not going to happen, sweetheart. I'm not sure what's going on between us, but whatever it is, it's good. I like it. I wouldn't hurt you like that."

"Okay."

His smile was tentative and a little sad. "I don't blame you for not trusting me, kitten. I'll work to change your mind."

"Look, Chase, I... I don't get why your brother did what he did. I know we don't fit together. I'm not the type of woman your family would pick. I get that. But he hurt me, and he did it on purpose. It shouldn't have bothered me, given our arrangement, but I'm gonna be honest here." She paused to inhale.

Chase prompted her to continue. "Okay."

"I know we have an agreement. I know you plan for us to go our separate ways after a year. I know that it's convenient to hang out with me, to   " She had to breathe again. "To sleep with me."

Throwing back his head, Chase laughed. There was a hint of self-deprecation hiding behind his obvious humor. "Kitten, there is *nothing* convenient about you."

Savannah didn't know how to take that. "Okay, fine. I'm inconvenient. Whatever. But just so you know, I don't sleep around. In fact, I can count the number of guys I've been with on one hand. I don't sleep with just anybody. But I slept with you. You remember that, Chase Barron. And you remember that I normally don't give second chances. I don't know if you just have bad luck or bad karma or bad...something. I won't be made a fool of. So no more chances. Don't blow what time we have left."

She shook free from his grasp, turned on her boot heel, tugged Cimarron's reins and stalked away. Chase watched, enjoying the angry sway of her hips far too much. Eventually, his brain lassoed his libido and he considered what she had—and hadn't—said. He'd admitted to Cash that he was in love with Savannah. Up until the moment she dropped his hand and walked away, he believed she was falling in love with him. Now he wasn't so sure.

Don't blow what time we have left.

She'd implied that she'd keep to their original agreement, that she'd divorce him after their year was up. That's what he wanted, too. Wasn't it? Given his family history, he was a bad bet in the marriage game. But something about Savannah called to him. She wasn't pretentious. She wasn't naive so much as guileless.

I can count the number of guys I've been with on one hand... But I slept with you. You remember that, Chase Barron.

Her words reverberated in his brain. She was the last person on this earth he should be involved with—much less be contemplating a long-term relationship with.

Knowing all of that didn't matter. He didn't care that she was wrong for him, because being with her felt too damn right. He had six months to change her mind. Less, actually. He had until December, when she returned to Las Vegas to compete in the Wrangler National Finals Rodeo. He was positive she'd be there. She'd be on his home turf, and he could make his move. He didn't need another chance. He was going to take the one he had and run with it.

Forget Operation Seduce Savannah. He was now all about Operation Rest of Our Lives, for better or worse.

His phone beeped with a text. He glanced at it. CALL ME!!! It was from Tucker, a man who never used all caps and thought exclamation points were for preteens texting about boy bands. His mind on ways to win his inconvenient cowgirl, Chase meandered to the arena and up to his box. Once seated, he texted Tucker back.

Little busy here. What's so important?

His phone rang almost immediately. He answered with "Not a good time, dude."

"Gonna have to make it a good time, cuz. The Feds are not happy you pitched a hissy and stormed out last night."

"Didn't have a choice, Tuck."

"Gonna enlighten me?"

"Cash."

"What about him?"

"He was here with Di Brandenburg."

"So?"

"Pretending to be me."

"Oh, crap. Savannah saw."

"Yeah."

"S'all good now?"

"Pretty much." Chase couldn't keep the smile out of his voice.

"Dang. Then this sucks. Sorry to burst your balloon, Chase, but I need you back here ASAP."

"No. I have plans with Savvie."

"I don't care. And neither do the Feds. This is a big deal, Chase. The fraud ring isn't just hitting us here in

Las Vegas. They hit the Barron Crown in Scottsdale last night. Palm Springs. Miami. They've all been targeted in the past few months."

"Why didn't we know?"

"No clue. Justice Department is wondering if we aren't helping them. Some sort of money laundering scheme or something."

"Well…hell."

"Look, I can probably stall them for a few days, but you need to get your butt back here as soon as you can."

"I'll fly back tomorrow. I want tonight with Savannah."

"Uh, Chase? What's the deal there?"

"It's the real deal, Tucker."

"You sure?"

"More than I've ever been. Being with her? It feels right, Tucker." Chase brushed his fingers through his hair and leaned forward, an elbow on his knee. Lowering his voice, he added, "Cash didn't take what I had to say very well."

"I can imagine."

"He set it up, Tuck." Anger leaked into his voice. "My own twin planned it out to hurt Savannah."

"That's low, cuz."

"Yeah." Silence stretched between them, though the arena came to life around him and crowd noise covered what he said next. "Something's wrong, Tuck."

"Yeah. The Feds are crawling all over us."

"I meant Cash, cuz. He's not…"

"He's not who you thought he was? You know, Chase, for a businessman as smart as you are, you sure wear blinders where your family is concerned. If your old man weren't my uncle—"

"What about Cash?"

"He's got a mean streak, Chase. He's always had it, even when we were kids. You got all the sunshine and rainbows. And Cash? Cash got the thunder and lightning."

Opening and closing his mouth several times as he attempted to form an answer, Chase finally gave up. "Not gonna discuss that now. Tell the Feds I'll be there tomorrow morning. Get with Bridger and find out what's been happening at our other properties. And get the accountants lined up. The Justice Department has wanted a piece of us ever since Clay won his first election."

Savannah took Chase to the airport the next morning. After dinner and dancing at one of the cowboy bars, they'd spent the night making love. She didn't want to say goodbye, afraid she'd lose something important if they were apart. They stood on the tarmac, Chase delaying getting on the plane as if he didn't want to go any more than she didn't want him to leave.

"Gonna miss you, kitten. And remember, if I text, I'll use our code word."

She was pretty sure she blushed to the roots of her hair. "*Purr* is not much of a code word, hoss."

"But you purr so prettily when I make you come."

Now she was positive her face was scarlet. "Shut up."

Chase laughed, a deep rolling sound from his chest. Wrapping his arms around her, he lifted her so they could kiss, then swung her around and around until she was giggling and dizzy. "Put me down, you big goof."

He did, though his hands lingered on her waist, and

he smiled down at her. "Can you make it home for a visit after Frontier Days?"

Savannah stilled at the word. *Home.* His home. The apartment in Vegas. Where he'd thrown her out of his bed, and then taken her to the heights of passion in that same bed. Moments passed and Chase squeezed her waist. She stammered out a breathless "Yes. I'll try."

He kissed her again, slowly, like she was some delicacy to be savored. She melted against him, her fingers curling in the lapels of his jacket. She rolled up on the balls of her feet to get closer to him, clinging just a little as he started to pull away. Part of her wanted to say the words, but she clamped her jaw shut as soon as she'd said, "I—"

"I?" Chase kissed the tip of her nose as she dropped back to stand flat-footed. "I what, kitten?"

She scrambled to fill in the blank. "Miss you. I will miss you." *A lot. A whole,* whole *lot.*

"Good. That means you'll be thinking about me. Turnabout is fair play, because I think about you all the time."

The flight attendant appeared in the doorway of the executive jet. "Sorry to interrupt, Mr. Barron, but the pilot says there's some weather moving in. We need to take off now to have any chance of missing it."

"I'll be right there." Chase turned back to Savannah. "Really gotta go, kitten. If you can't make it to Vegas, I'll see you in Dodge City." He flashed her a lopsided grin with a hint of dimple and a wink. "Provided Dodge City has an airport."

She sputtered in support of Dodge. "For a man born and raised in Oklahoma, that's just mean. Dodge City is awesome."

"It is when you're there." He glanced over his shoulder and waved at the flight attendant. "Gotta go, babe. Call me."

"Ditto. You, me."

They kissed one last time until Chase broke away. He paused at the door to the plane and waved. Savannah backed up, but waited, waving at him until the plane taxied away.

Savannah didn't go to Vegas between rodeos. Chase had to fly to Miami. He didn't join her in Dodge City. Or Caldwell, Idaho. Something related to his business always came up. Savannah would have been angry or hurt, but Chase called her constantly. He even bought her an iPad so they could Skype, and she could respond to his sexy emails. And oh, boy, did he send sexy emails. She would read them and blush, and then the ornery cuss would tag her on Skype just so he could see her face.

Deep down, Savannah knew he wasn't avoiding her, despite evidence to the contrary. Even Tucker vouched for him. So she did what she'd always done. She drove from rodeo to rodeo. She competed. She mostly won, sometimes lost and learned she could call Chase when she was feeling down. He never failed to take her call. If he was in the middle of a meeting, he took a moment to talk to her, and then set a time when they could Skype.

September rolled around and that meant the Pendleton Round-up. Like Calgary and Cheyenne, Pendleton was one of the big ones. It was an important rodeo with the stiffest competition. Winning at Pendleton was a big deal, but she was so lonely, she could barely get out of bed.

Staring at the mirror in her hotel room, she reminded herself of her idiotic tendencies. "He's a busy man, Savannah. He runs a huge corporation. And you're just his…" She stopped speaking as she considered what exactly she was. What had he said all those months ago when he proposed this? A marriage of convenience. "That's all you are, girl. Just a convenient wife. Yeah, he likes the stuff we do in bed. He probably even likes you. But forever? Nope. When the year's up, he'll be done with you, ready to move on."

She made good time in the afternoon run. Her evening run was even better. She was in Cimarron's stall, brushing him down, when she looked up. Chase stood in the stall door, a half smile on his face and something she couldn't describe in his eyes.

"I remember standing in a stall like this in Vegas, watching you worry over a horse. Watching you straighten your shoulders when the world tried to slam you to the ground." His quiet voice washed over her, filling the empty spaces that had opened up in his absence. He stepped in, closed the gate behind him. He took the curry brush from her hand, tossed it into the bucket in the corner of the stall. "I've missed you, kitten."

Savannah fell into his arms. "You're here. You…" She cupped his cheeks and kissed him. "You're really here." She closed her eyes as she laid her head against his shoulder, hoping to stem the relieved tears forming there.

"I'm really here. And if my brother Chance hadn't warned me about making love on straw, I'd show you just how excited I am. But you have a big, comfortable bed in your hotel room, yeah?"

"Yeah." She grinned at him as his eyes grew hooded and that dang dimple came out to play.

"Yeah."

Oh, the things her man could say with only one syllable.

Twenty

Vegas. She was in Vegas. Savannah's emotions were as crazy as a Tilt-a-Whirl. She'd made the National Finals. As a top-fifteen money winner, she was one of the last cowgirls standing in the race to the All-Around Cowgirl Championship. She'd done it. Being here was exciting, the culmination of everything she'd worked for since her first win, at the rodeo held in conjunction with the Western National Stock Show in Denver last January. October and November had been nuts—totally crazypants with back-to-back rodeos as she pushed to make the cut for the NFR.

Vegas. Yeah, but. She was in Vegas. In Chase's home. Well, his apartment atop the Crown Hotel and Casino. With a whole rack of her clothes in the closet, most of which still had the price tags attached. All of which she'd stared at for almost an hour, trying to decide what to wear. Chase wanted her to go with him to Barron House for dinner with an associate and his fiancée.

"I want to show you off," he'd said.

Which made her panic. She almost broke out in hives just thinking about the Barron House. She couldn't stall any longer—not if she was going to be on time. There was no way she'd be late—even fashionably. So her emotions had run away to the carnival and were currently riding every scary ride on the midway.

Savannah twisted off her wedding band and grimaced. No matter how often she cleaned her hands, the black mark continued to encircle her ring finger. She tried not to let it bother her. She really did. But after their wedding, especially when their relationship went to new levels of commitment, she'd figured he'd buy her a real ring. Except he hadn't. In fact, he hadn't bought her any jewelry at all—not that she wore much, but still. It was the principle. Drying her hands and slipping the cheap ring back on her finger, she tried not to think about waking up the morning after their completely Vegas-style wedding and having to face Chase's father. Then there was that scene with the maître d' at the restaurant—the one his father had witnessed.

She smoothed her palms down the coffee-brown microsuede skirt she'd chosen to wear. Paneled, it hugged her curves yet still swirled around the pair of custom-stitched boots on her feet. She'd dithered—and wasn't that a fun word to describe the near-panicked freak-out she endured while picking out an outfit to wear. She eventually breathed through it and chose a cashmere sweater the color of butterscotch to go with the skirt.

With the addition of a turquoise-and-silver squash blossom necklace and a fringed shawl, she figured even the snooty maître d' would be impressed. The still-vivid memory of that encounter plagued her all the way down in the elevator.

With more confidence than she felt, Savannah wended her way through the main floor of the hotel to reach the restaurant. She slowed when the front entrance came into view. If Chase arrived first, would he wait for her? Or would he already be seated at his table with the couple? Was she late? She glanced at her watch. No. She was a few minutes early. Breathing deeply, she controlled her emotions. She was Mrs. Chase Barron. She could do this.

Approaching the host stand, she plastered a smile on her face, all the while rehearsing what she was going to say. *Good evening, I'm Mrs. Barron. Is my husband's table set up for our guests? Good evening, I'm Mrs. Barron—*

"You have some nerve."

The cutting voice interrupted her thoughts and her forward momentum. She'd been so wrapped up in getting through the next few minutes, she'd totally tuned out everything around her. But when she looked up, she found herself face-to-face with Cyrus Barron. She scrambled to collect her thoughts. Was he supposed to be there for the meeting? Had Chase told her and had she blanked it out?

"Excuse me?"

"You heard me. You have no class and no sense of

propriety. Parading around pretending to be married to my son."

"She is married to your *son,* old man. I don't recall inviting you to dinner after the meeting this afternoon."

Chase. He'd come up behind her and even now ignored his father to smile at her, his eyes warm and appreciative as he took in her outfit. He dropped a kiss on her mouth, careful not to smear her lipstick.

"Don't kiss that woman in public."

Chase narrowed his eyes at his father's derogatory emphasis on the word *woman.* "Don't go there, old man." He stepped in front of Savannah, partially shielding her, acutely aware that his father had bushwhacked her.

"We're done, Dad. You don't get to do this to my wife. You don't get to do this to me."

"Shut up, Chasen. You listen to me, boy—"

"I am not your *boy.* I am the CEO of Barron Entertainment. I run this hotel and ten others. I oversee radio and television stations and a whole group of other entertainment enterprises. I make this family a ton of money. I've worked my butt off to get where I am and you will respect me as the corporate officer who made that happen even if you don't respect me as your son."

His anger made him reckless and he pressed closer to his father. "I get it now."

Cyrus's eyes widened, but he leaned toward Chase. "Get what?"

"Why our family sucks. Two things are gonna happen now. Either you apologize to Savannah and return to your table, or I will have you escorted out by Security and banned from this property." To emphasize his statement, Chase eased Savannah to his side, his arm around her shoulders in a show of support.

"You've made your bed, boy." He flicked his gaze over Savannah. In a voice as cold and insincere as he was, Cyrus added, "My apologies."

Chase turned Savannah into his chest, both arms around her. He rubbed the top of her head with his chin and murmured, "My old man is a jackass, kitten. I'll make sure you're never alone with him again. Okay?"

"Okay."

Holding her hand, he brushed past the maître d', who stood there as still as a statue. "I have two guests coming. Mr. Brown and his companion. Show them to my table when they get here."

"Yes, sir. Of course, Mr. Barron."

He seated Savannah at their table, ordered wine for her and a Scotch neat for himself. After the waiter disappeared, he took her hand and pulled it onto his thigh under the table. "Breathe, kitten. You're fine." He let his appreciation for her beauty bleed into his expression. "And gorgeous." He fingered the sleeve of her sweater. "Soft. Like the woman wearing it."

And there was the pink tingeing her cheeks that he so enjoyed. No one had ever spoiled this woman, had ever told her she was beautiful and cherished. He had plans to do both for a very long time. But the waiter came back with the drinks just as the other members of their party arrived, interrupting him. After a round of introductions and then everyone ordering dinner, Chase settled in, his arm around the back of Savannah's chair while he turned his attention to Jason Brown. Brown fancied himself a corporate raider, and the man had his eye on one of the Barron properties. If the price was right, Chase would do business, but that *if* was a huge question mark at the moment.

Savannah, still shaken from her encounter with her father-in-law, did her best to entertain Heather with the last name she couldn't remember. During introductions, she'd learned that Heather and Jason's wedding was imminent. During their meal, she discovered that Heather couldn't speak or eat without waving her left hand. The huge diamond nestled in a pile of big diamonds glittered in the light cast by flames dancing in the nearby fireplace. Savvie was duly impressed— what woman wouldn't be? Still, she was getting fed up with Heather flaunting her ring.

Chase and Jason were deep in a discussion about cost overruns and acceptable losses. Savannah tuned in to them. Even though she didn't really understand the terminology, the men's conversation was infinitely more interesting than Heather's incessant wedding chatter.

"What about yours?"

Savannah jerked her attention back to the other woman. "Excuse me?"

"Your ring?" Heather huffed out a breath to indicate her irritation. "I was asking about your wedding ring." She made a dismissive gesture by flicking her bediamonded hand toward Savannah's left hand.

Glancing down, Savannah just managed to hide her wince. The dark circle left on her skin by the cheap metal was clearly visible again.

"Considering how much the Barrons are worth, I figured you'd have double the number of carats as I have in my ring. At a minimum."

Embarrassed, Savannah struggled to hold on to her composure even as Jason chastised his fiancée.

"Seriously, Heather? We discussed this." Jason turned to Chase, who kept his gaze focused on Savannah. "I'm sorry, Chase. Heather and her sorority sisters have this whole mine's-better gamesmanship going on. I've cautioned her that not everyone is as concerned about quality or quantity as she is."

Savannah couldn't meet Chase's intense stare, wishing the floor would open up and swallow her.

Heather huffed out a breath, ignoring Savannah and focusing on her fiancé. "But look at her hand, Jason. That ring is just…cheap." The woman pitched her voice just loud enough that the large group seated nearby, and Cyrus Barron, turned to watch.

Chase reached over and clasped her left hand. He lifted it, staring intently while he rubbed his thumb over her ring finger, before raising her hand to his mouth for a kiss. Then he turned the intensity of his stare on Heather.

"I'm a very lucky man, Ms. Martin. My wife is a cowgirl. She has her priorities straight. Savannah is also sentimental. There's a story behind this ring and she wears it to remind me what's important." He raised his free hand and their waiter appeared immediately. "Add twenty-five percent to the tab for your tip, Kirk."

He pushed back from the table, still holding Savannah's hand for a moment. Then he released her so he could hold her chair as she stood to join him. "I think we're done, Jason. Ms. Martin, I wish I could say it was a pleasure."

Chase didn't wait for a response from the couple. He tucked Savannah's hand into the crook of his elbow and walked out of the restaurant with her. Cyrus caught up to them.

"When are you going to come to your senses and end this travesty of a marriage?"

"Shut up, old man." Chase's hand clenched around hers as she stiffened beside him.

Smirking, Cyrus shook his head. The smirk morphed into a coldly deliberate sneer. "You won't win, Chase."

Savannah could breathe again at Chase's next words.

"I already have."

Twenty-One

Savannah was floating on air—or would be if she wasn't riding Cimarron. She'd done it! Champion All-Around Cowgirl! She even had the belt buckle to prove it. And the saddle. And the prize money. The endorsements. The trailer. Not that she needed one, considering Chase's generosity. She couldn't wait to see him, to fall into his arms for a big hug and a searing kiss. He'd be proud of her, proud *for* her. Ever since the night he'd stood up for her, taking on his father on her behalf, their relationship had deepened. Tonight, they were both winners.

Chase talked about *when*. *When* they went here, *when* they did this or that. He spoke in future terms and never with an *if.* Convinced he wanted a future with her, believing he shared the same feelings for her that she held for him, she'd let her guard down. She'd opened her heart and welcomed him with open arms and unconditionally. She loved him. She'd admitted that to herself in Cheyenne after the thought of him being with another woman left her devastated and so angry she couldn't breathe between the sobs.

In the months following, he'd done everything in his power to show her how much he cared. He'd gotten her to trust him. And she was ready to be honest and tell him how she felt about him. Coming out of the arena after accepting her awards, she'd expected him to be behind the chutes waiting for her. He wasn't.

She pulled her phone from her hip pocket. No text. No missed call. Concern now colored her excitement. Dismounting, she led the big paint horse to the competitors' holding area. She could put him in a stall while she searched out Chase. She knew he was here. She'd seen him before her last run, had seen him in his box cheering as she rode into the arena to collect her prizes when she was announced the winner.

Standing, unsure of what to do or where to go, Savannah was surprised when one of the candidates for rodeo queen sauntered by with an insincere smile on her face. Great. Just who she wanted to run into. Twyla Allan, the same girl who'd been draped all over Chase back at the Clark County rodeo right after her marriage.

Twyla stopped and with a catty look on her face asked, "Looking for that gorgeous hunk you claim is your man?"

Something about the other girl's demeanor worried Savannah, but she nodded her head, unable to stop the gesture.

"Saw him back that way, headed toward the competitors' lounge."

"Oh. Uh, thanks." Savannah walked away but glanced back over her shoulder to find Twyla watching her go, a hand on one hip, her eyes smoldering and a smirk crinkling her lips. Something was wrong. Like the chick knew something Savannah didn't. That was bad. Very bad.

All but trotting, she jogged past the holding pens. People clogged the area behind the chutes and she ended up playing running back as she dodged and cut between cowboys, officials and others. She waved off shouted congratulations with a distracted smile and hand flick. The closer she got to the area under the arena where the hospitality room was located, the more panicked she became.

One of the bigwigs with Wrangler jeans caught her, staying her forward progress with a hand on her arm. He wanted to talk about a sponsorship. Accepting his card, with a promise to call, she rushed on. The leather soles of her boots slipped on the incline leading from the staging area floor up to the first level, where hospitality was located. She reached the landing and made a sliding turn. When she regained her balance, she stopped dead at the sound of Chase's laughter. His deep, sexy, only-for-her laughter.

He stood twenty feet away, surrounded by paparazzi he'd most likely tweeted to get there. A curvy, blonde cowgirl stood on his left. She had her arm around his neck and his hand rested comfortably on her hip. The Stetson on her head was tipped back, and she was laughing at what Chase was saying. The camera flashes lit up the hallway as though it was the Fourth of July. A second woman stood tucked against his right side. Her thick hair was a dark chestnut with red highlights. She was as gorgeous as the blonde, and her hand was splayed across Chase's abs.

Savannah's stomach cramped and she had to bend over, her hands braced on her thighs. Two women. Both beautiful. And definitely cowgirls from the way they were dressed. Real cowgirls, not the kind who would shop in Leather and Lace.

Somebody tapped her on the shoulder, and she jerked upright. Twyla.

"Just wanted to check to make sure you're all right, hon."

Yeah, Savannah just bet she did. She straightened without looking at the girl with the tiara attached to her cowboy hat. "I'm fine, Twyla. Just a little light-headed from all the congratulations."

"Sure, whatever. Anyway, I see you found your *husband*."

She didn't need to see Twyla's face. Savannah heard the sneer in the way she said that last word. "I did, and now you can get lost." She didn't add the name she wanted to call the pushy, two-faced witch.

"Now, why would I want to do that? You think you're all that because you conned Chase into marrying you. What you see is what you get, and I get to watch you getting it." Twyla cackled, her glee evident.

What you see is what you get. She'd believed him in Cheyenne, that his brother had masqueraded as Chase. But what if the twins had pulled a double switch? What if Chase had actually stayed in Cheyenne for the rendezvous with Di and Cash had been here in Vegas dealing with those federal officers? Oh, yeah, they could have pulled that off.

She blanked her face. No way would she give Twyla

the satisfaction of seeing her crumble. She was Savannah Wolfe and she would keep her chin up. No freaking matter what. Her brain whirled. Should she confront him? Should she just walk up as though she had no problem he was all but making out with two beautiful women? Should she walk away, go back to the hotel and eviscerate him in private?

The decision was made for her when the blonde turned and saw her standing in the hall. The woman leaned closer to Chase and whispered in his ear, her eyes never leaving Savannah. That's when Savannah knew. That's when she saw the same look on the blonde's face as she'd seen on Di Brandenburg's. That's when she knew she'd been played for a fool. Frozen in place a moment too long, she watched Chase's head turn. Saw him recognize her. Saw the moment he understood he'd blown it with her. She watched him shake off the women, watched him take a few steps in her direction, fighting through the throng of reporters.

That's when her muscles thawed and her brain took over. She pivoted and ducked back down the ramp. By the time she hit level ground, she was sprinting. Cimarron. She'd leave him. He was safe in the pen. She'd call Kade later to come pick him up. Him and Red. She didn't want them. She didn't want the trailer. The clothes. Nothing. At the moment, though, what she wanted was to get away. Needed to get away. Someone called her name. She kept running.

Chase lost sight of Savannah in the crowd. People were staring, but that didn't matter. All he cared about was getting to Savvie, explaining to her. The look on her face had gutted him. She believed he'd betrayed her. He had to talk to her. Tell her he was an idiot. That what she saw wasn't what she thought it was.

"Chase! What the hell, bud?" Chance grabbed his shoulder and forced him to stop.

Cord stood next to Chance, breathing hard. "You almost knocked Jolie down. Not cool, dude."

A moment later, Clay pushed through the mass of people, sheltering Georgie against his side, while he made a path for Cassidy and Jolie. "Want to explain what that mad dash was all about?"

Chase stared at his brothers and their wives. He knew Savannah had seen him with them. Knew she'd leaped to the wrong conclusion. And he knew why. He'd never introduced her to his family. To anyone besides Tucker. Just as he'd been thoughtless about that cheap ring he'd put on her finger, he'd never considered taking her home to Oklahoma to meet his brothers and their wives. To meet Miz Beth and Big John, the caretakers who'd all but raised the Barron boys. He'd made her his wife but he hadn't made her part of his family. He'd planned to remedy that, but he'd waited too long.

Cassidy sidled up beside Chance. "Why did she freak out like that, Chase?"

The question was a legitimate one. He'd told no one but Tucker about Cash's sabotage attempt in Cheyenne. Why he'd felt the need to protect his twin was beyond his comprehension at the moment. Cash had done despicable things to all of them.

Hunter Tate, Clay's chief of security, appeared, along with several of the Tate brothers and a man Chase vaguely recognized as part of Clay's security team. His oldest brother was a US senator and had been campaigning for the presidency before following his heart to marry Georgie, Clay's former director of communications. The football scrum of Barrons and Tates put the three ladies in the middle and moved outside to the parking lot, where they had a modicum of privacy.

Jolie fisted her hands on her hips and did her best to look tough. The ER nurse got right to the point. "Just say it, Chase. Rip the Band-Aid off fast."

Chase watched Clay shrug off his leather jacket and drape it around Georgie's shoulders. She was still recovering from the illness that threatened her life. The tenderness in that gesture floored Chase. He wanted that with Savannah. Inhaling deeply to fortify his resolve, he laid it out for his family.

"Chance knows most of the story. The beginning, anyway. Dad decided I needed to get married. He picked out Janiece Carroll. Tucker got wind of things." He glanced around the group and realized Kade had joined them. The ranch manager did not look happy. "Since I was supposed to be out of town, Kade arranged to have Savannah stay in my apartment. Only I came home early. And kicked her out."

He dropped his chin at that admission. "In my defense," he told the pavement, "I'd just gotten burned by those two singers in Nashville."

"So you made amends by marrying her?" Kade's voice betrayed his tightly held anger.

"We made a deal. She needed help. I needed a wife. It was convenient for both of us."

"Convenient?" Cassie brushed a slap against the back of his head. "What were you thinkin'? Oh, wait. You weren't thinking. Duh."

"This doesn't explain why we're standing here in

the middle of a parking lot on a chilly December night, little bro." Cord always cut to the heart of the matter.

"I discovered I liked her. A lot. And then I fell in love with her."

No one said a word. He couldn't even hear them breathing. He glanced up. Every one of them wore the same shocked expression. "You heard me. I fell in love."

He went on to explain about Cash. About his father. The ring. His idea to have them all there when he presented her with a real ring and asked Savannah to spend the rest of her life with him. He finished up with "And in true Barron fashion, I've totally screwed up everything."

"Ya think?" Cassie rolled her eyes. "Dude, you really shot yourself in the foot this time. We need to fix this."

Chance reeled her into his side with an arm around her neck. "No, sweetheart, *Chase* needs to fix this."

Twenty-Two

"Where would she go?" Chase considered the question, not realizing he'd voiced it aloud until Cord snorted.

"You're asking us? Like we'd have a clue because we know her so well."

He glared at his brother. "Yeah, stick that knife in and twist, Cord. My fault I didn't introduce her to y'all. My fault she didn't realize who Cass and Jolie are. My fault." His voice rose with each sentence he uttered and he finished by throwing his hands in the air.

"Where's her old truck?"

Clay focused on Kade. "What?"

"She left Cimarron in a holding pen. Big Red is in his stall. The trailer hasn't moved. I had Security check, and her new truck is gone. That surprises me. I figured she would have left it and taken a cab."

"What are you sayin', Kade?"

"I'm sayin' that I know Sav. She'll walk away from everything you gave her." He shoved his thumbs in the front pockets of his jeans. "Let me ask you this. What's in your apartment? The stuff she owns, I mean."

Chase considered, mentally walking through the closet. "Her clothes. Her…stuff."

"All of her clothes? Her duffel bag?"

He searched his memory again. Thought about what she'd taken the first time she tried to run. "Ah, hell." He stared at Kade. "She kept the stuff she arrived with in that duffel."

"Yup. And she keeps that duffel in the truck. She'll walk away with exactly what she walked in with." Kade's eyes hardened. "And she'll walk away from the money she won this year. She'll consider the winnings payback for your sponsorship."

"Ah, hell."

Tucker's phone pinged and he glanced at the screen before accepting the call. He held up a finger as he listened. "No. Don't do anything. Just keep an eye on her. We'll be there shortly." He returned his gaze to Chase. "She's in the parking garage at the Crown."

Chase breathed around the tightness in his chest. "She's gone home."

Kade growled in frustration. "No, you idiot. She doesn't have a home. Except that damn ol' Ford pickup of hers."

Hunt stepped closer, his phone in his hand. "SUVs will be here in a minute. We'll load up and head her off."

Chase had VIP parking and his Jag was close. "I can't wait."

* * *

Savannah finally found her old pickup. Breathing heavily, she leaned against its rusty fender and bit her lip to stave off her tears. Her hands shook even though she pressed them against the hood. Her nose burned and her vision was blurry. This corner of the hotel's parking garage was cloaked in shadows. No one could see her. No one would know that Chase's betrayal shattered her heart into so many pieces she'd never find them all.

Stiffening her spine, she pushed off the hood and stood straight. She was better than that. Stronger. She wasn't her mother. She didn't need a man to define her. Support her. Take care of her. She'd been taking care of herself since she was twelve. Wiping her sleeve over her cheeks, she squared her shoulders.

She was done with anything bearing the Barron name, including the prenup, checking account and her winnings, all bought and paid for by Chase. She couldn't keep any of it and walk away with her pride intact.

She had to dump the contents of her purse to find the keys to the old Ford. She unlocked it and transferred her belongings from the new truck. She'd leave the key with the security guard at the exit. Settling in behind the steering wheel of her Ford, she inserted the key in the ignition and turned it.

Nothing happened.

No click. No whirr. No grinding chug. Nothing. And didn't that just sum up her life? She had nothing but a couple pairs of worn blue jeans, some old shirts, a pair of boots she didn't pay for but was keeping because she didn't want to go barefoot and a heap of a truck that wouldn't even start.

In the distance, she heard the rumble of life on the Strip. Closer, tires squealed as a driver took the circular ramp too fast. She got out, popped the hood. Everything looked okay. She jiggled the wires on the battery. Back in the driver's seat, she cranked the ignition. Nothing. Just like her. Her mother had been right—she was a loser. At least Chase had listened and not paid her old lady a cent. Savannah slumped, her forehead resting on the steering wheel as she let the tears fall.

Tires screeched right in front of her, and she looked up to see Chase's Jaguar blocking her truck. She had just enough presence of mind to slam her door and lock it. He stalked to her, but she couldn't decipher the expression on his face. Anger. Hurt. Concern. At the moment, anger was the primary emotion.

He jerked the door handle and his face clouded. "Open the door, Savannah."

"No."

He jerked again, then pounded on the window. "Open the damn door, Sav."

"No!"

More vehicles arrived. Black SUVs. People climbed out. She watched, slightly disconnected from the scene. Chase continued to bang on the window and shout.

"Open the door or I'll break the window."

Three women appeared—the blonde, the auburn-haired beauty and a third woman with short hair. They were accompanied by three men. Savannah blinked. She recognized Senator Clay Barron. His arm encircled the short-haired woman. Savvie swallowed hard. She vaguely remembered some news reports about

Clay stopping his presidential campaign to be with his fiancée while she fought cancer. Savannah's gaze tracked to the other two women, and the men with them. She didn't recognize the men beyond the fact that they had to be Barrons. Chase's brothers?

"Dammit, Savvie! Swear to God I'm gonna rip this door off if you don't open it right now."

What was going on? She popped the lock, and in less than a breath, Chase had jerked the door open and pulled her out. He gripped her biceps and shook her.

"What were you thinking? Why did you run away?"

Her gaze remained glued on the two women. "I saw you."

"I know, kitten. But you didn't *see*."

"Yes, I did."

"No, you didn't. You saw what you wanted to see, not what was really there." He inhaled sharply and backed up, tugging her with him. "This is not the way I wanted to do this. Not the way I planned. At. All." He pointed to the women. "My sisters-in-law. Cassidy Barron. She's married to my brother Chance. That's Jolie. She married Cord and is the mother of my favorite nephew."

Cord snorted. "CJ is your only nephew, bud."

"You didn't see her back at the arena, but that's Georgie, who is Clay's wife."

"Uh-huh."

"Uh-huh? That's all you have to say?" He stormed away several steps and turned back. "You didn't trust me, Savannah. How can I do this if you don't trust me?"

She gulped, and as she often did when nervous, rubbed her thumb against the cheap metal of the band on her left ring finger. She opened her mouth to defend herself, but Chase didn't give her the chance.

"Look, I know I screwed up. Royally. From the beginning. I take responsibility for that. But I also made you a promise. And I asked you to trust me. At the first sign of trouble—perceived trouble—you cut and run. Do you really believe I'm such a bastard that I'd throw women in your face?"

She hung her head. "I'm sorry."

"Ah, Savannah." His voice broke as he gathered her into his arms. Stroking her back, Chase murmured against her hair, "I'm the one who's sorry, kitten. I'm a jerk. I admit that. I should have introduced you to my family. I should have gotten you a real ring. I should have taken better care of you. I…" He cleared the lump in his throat. "I'm the world's biggest idiot but I swear I never meant to hurt you."

He loosened his arms and dropped to one knee. "I didn't do this the first time I asked. But you deserve this." He dug in his pocket and pulled out a velvet box. Snapping it open, he removed the rings nestled inside. "I'm asking you for real this time. In front of my family. I love you, Savannah Wolfe Barron. Love you with my whole heart. Will you marry me again? I want you. Now and forever. I want you to have my last name. I want to live with you. Love you. Fight with you. Make up with you. Because I can promise, me being me? I'm always gonna screw up somehow."

Everything faded into the distance as she focused on him. His expression said it all—soft, pleading eyes, hesitant smile. She cupped his cheeks, bent to kiss him.

"Yes," she whispered.

Chase surged to his feet, grabbed her and swung

her in a circle. Then he removed the old ring, slipped it in his pocket, and placed the new engagement ring and wedding band on her finger.

"I love you, hoss."

"Not as much as I love you, kitten."

And he did. He loved his inconvenient cowgirl with his whole heart.

Epilogue

"You sure about this, cuz?"

Chase gazed at Tucker a full minute before rolling his eyes. "Seriously? You ask me this now?"

Tuck clapped him on the back, sloshing the coffee in his cup. "Better now than later."

He watched his best friend's expression morph from teasing to serious. "I'm happy for you, Chase. You know that, right? She's good for you."

"Yeah, I know. She's… I don't know how to explain how she makes me feel."

"That's good, because really? Dude, we're guys. We don't talk about that stuff." Tucker shuddered dramatically. "Feelings. Ugh!"

Laughing, Chase glanced around to see his brothers entering the family great room. A huge Christmas tree filled the corner near the massive fireplace. Miz Beth had outdone herself. For the first time in a long time, Chase was happy to be in Oklahoma to celebrate the holidays with his family, especially since Cyrus had chosen Hawaii and a female companion over being here. For the first time in ages, this felt like home. And he had Savannah to thank for that.

"Welcome to the ranks, little bro." Cord wrapped an arm around Chase's neck and gave him a short, strangling hug.

"Glad you found her," Clay added. "And didn't let her get away."

Chance studied him a moment. "It's good to see you happy, little bro."

Looking at Clay, Cord and Chance, Chase realized one face was missing. Cash. His twin. They'd parted on angry words last summer in Cheyenne, and Cash had avoided him since.

More laughing male voices crowded in. Tucker's brothers had arrived, stomping in from the kitchen. Barrons and Tates. One big, dysfunctional family where blood always tied them together. His sisters-in-law appeared, laughing at something. He watched as they picked out their husbands in the crowd. Georgie, still looking wan but getting healthier every day, didn't have to go far. Clay was beside her immediately, tucking her under his arm.

CJ, his nephew, hit Cord like a mini tornado. Jolie had eyes only for her men—Cord and CJ. By the time she reached them, Cord had his son up on a hip as he reached for his wife and pulled her in for a kiss.

Cassidy, all sass and hair tossing, sashayed to Chance and rolled up to her tiptoes to kiss him. He held her a moment, then turned her so her back rested against his front, his arms crossed over her chest.

"Savannah's almost dressed," Cass announced to the room at large. She turned to Chase, her eyes twinkling with mischief as the doorbell rang. "You should get that, Chase."

Suspicious, Chase prowled to the front door. He opened it and discovered a lavender-haired Liberace in a fur coat standing there with Kade. Kade got his big foot wedged in the door before Chase could slam it shut.

"No. Not happening!" Chase was adamant. Laughter spilled out from the other room. Almost all of his family was here. But a moment of isolation stabbed through him. He wanted Cash to be here, too, despite everything.

Kade urged the Liberace impersonator inside and shut the door behind them. "Dude's not licensed in Oklahoma, but since y'all are already married, doesn't matter. He's gonna say the words again." He glanced around. "Where's my girl?"

"Up here." Savannah's voice floated down from the landing at the top of the stairs, arcing over the foyer.

Chase couldn't breathe. Her black hair fell in thick waves around her face, over her shoulders and down her back. Brown eyes shining, her face glowing with happiness, she stepped down. She wore a long skirt that looked like lace, only…it wasn't. The cream-colored crocheted skirt brushed the toes of her boots. She lifted it to descend, and Chase saw that her Western boots were the color of red dirt. A matching leather belt cinched her hips and he recognized the heavy silver buckle—her All-Around Cowgirl Championship buckle. A silk blouse the color of the Oklahoma sky caressed her curves and his fingers itched to mold the material to her skin.

"Beautiful." That's what his mouth said, but his brain? His brain was shouting, *MINE!*

He met her at the bottom step and took her hand. Together, they returned to the great room. With family gathered around, Liberace read the words that would renew their vows. Chase took them to heart this time. For better or worse. In sickness and in health. Until death did them part. His inconvenient cowgirl was now the most important person in his life. He looked around the room, his gaze connecting with each of his brothers and their wives. Chase understood now, understood where his big brothers found the strength to stand up for themselves and the women they loved.

Movement near the arch leading to the kitchen caught his attention. Whoever stood there didn't come into the family room, but Chase knew who it was, knew the shape of that shadow as well as he did his own. Cash had come home, after all. Chase sent a look and a barely perceptible nod that direction. No one else saw, but his twin would.

"You may now kiss your bride."

Chase gathered Savannah into his arms and she tipped up on her toes as he lowered his head to kiss her. "I love you." They spoke simultaneously, their words and breath mingling. And he realized some things the moment she melted into his arms for the kiss that sealed their lives. He did need a wife, so long as it was this woman. And blood wasn't what tied a family together. It was love.

* * * * *

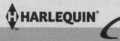

REQUEST YOUR FREE BOOKS!
2 FREE NOVELS PLUS 2 FREE GIFTS!

ⒽHARLEQUIN®

Desire

ALWAYS POWERFUL, PASSIONATE AND PROVOCATIVE

YES! Please send me 2 FREE Harlequin® Desire novels and my 2 FREE gifts (gifts are worth about $10). After receiving them, if I don't wish to receive any more books, I can return the shipping statement marked "cancel." If I don't cancel, I will receive 6 brand-new novels every month and be billed just $4.55 per book in the U.S. or $5.24 per book in Canada. That's a savings of at least 13% off the cover price! It's quite a bargain! Shipping and handling is just 50¢ per book in the U.S. and 75¢ per book in Canada.* I understand that accepting the 2 free books and gifts places me under no obligation to buy anything. I can always return a shipment and cancel at any time. Even if I never buy another book, the two free books and gifts are mine to keep forever.

225/326 HDN GH2P

Name _____ (PLEASE PRINT) _____

Address _____ Apt. # _____

City _____ State/Prov. _____ Zip/Postal Code _____

Signature (if under 18, a parent or guardian must sign) _____

Mail to the **Reader Service:**
IN U.S.A.: P.O. Box 1867, Buffalo, NY 14240-1867
IN CANADA: P.O. Box 609, Fort Erie, Ontario L2A 5X3

Want to try two free books from another line?
Call 1-800-873-8635 or visit www.ReaderService.com.

* Terms and prices subject to change without notice. Prices do not include applicable taxes. Sales tax applicable in N.Y. Canadian residents will be charged applicable taxes. Offer not valid in Quebec. This offer is limited to one order per household. Not valid for current subscribers to Harlequin Desire books. All orders subject to credit approval. Credit or debit balances in a customer's account(s) may be offset by any other outstanding balance owed by or to the customer. Please allow 4 to 6 weeks for delivery. Offer available while quantities last.

Your Privacy—The Reader Service is committed to protecting your privacy. Our Privacy Policy is available online at www.ReaderService.com or upon request from the Reader Service.

We make a portion of our mailing list available to reputable third parties that offer products we believe may interest you. If you prefer that we not exchange your name with third parties, or if you wish to clarify or modify your communication preferences, please visit us at www.ReaderService.com/consumerchoice or write to us at Reader Service Preference Service, P.O. Box 9062, Buffalo, NY 14240-9062. Include your complete name and address.

HDI5

"Are you going to suggest that I need *you*?" she asked,
her voice choked.

Lightning streaked through his blood, and in that
moment, he was lost. It didn't matter that he thought
she was insufferable, a prissy little princess who didn't
appreciate anything she had. It didn't matter that he was
up here to work.

All that mattered was he hadn't touched a woman in a
long time, and Madison West was so close all he would
have to do was shift his weight slightly and he'd be able
to take her into his arms.

"Well," he said, "you have a couple of the essential
ingredients to have yourself a pretty fun evening. All you
seem to be missing is a good man. I'm not very nice,
Madison," he said, leaning in, "but I could damn sure
show you a good time."

She should throw him out. She looked over at him, and her libido made a dash to the foreground. That was the problem. He irritated her. He was exactly the kind of man she didn't like. He was cocky; he was rough and crude. However, there was something about the way he looked in a tight T-shirt that made a mockery of all that very certain hatred.

"Are you going to take off your coat and stay awhile?" That question, asked in a faintly mocking tone, sent a dart of tension straight down between her thighs.

She could *not* take off her coat. Because she was wearing nothing more than a little scrap of red lace underneath it. And now it was all she could think of. "It's cold," she snapped. "Maybe if you went to work getting the electricity back on rather than standing here making terrible double entendres I would be able to take off my coat."

The maddening man raised his eyebrows, shooting her a look that clearly said Suit yourself, then set about looking for the fuse box. She let out an exasperated sigh and followed his path, stopping when she saw him leaning against the wall, a little metal door between the logs open as he examined the switches inside.

"It's not a fuse. That means there's something else going on." He slammed the door shut and turned back to look at her. "You should come over to my cabin."

Don't miss
HOLD ME, COWBOY
by New York Times *bestselling author Maisey Yates,*
available November 2016 wherever
Harlequin® Desire books and ebooks are sold.

www.Harlequin.com

HDEXP1016R

Whatever You're Into... Passionate Reads

Looking for more passionate reads from Harlequin®?
Fear not! Harlequin® Presents, Harlequin® Desire and
Harlequin® Blaze offer you irresistible romance stories
featuring powerful heroes.

⬥HARLEQUIN *Presents.*

Do you want alpha males, decadent glamour and jet-set
lifestyles? Step into the sensational, sophisticated world of
Harlequin® Presents, where sinfully tempting heroes ignite a
fierce and wickedly irresistible passion!

⬥HARLEQUIN *Desire*

Harlequin® Desire novels are powerful, passionate and
provocative contemporary romances set against a backdrop of
wealth, privilege and sweeping family saga. Alpha heroes with
a soft side meet strong-willed but vulnerable heroines amid a
dramatic world of divided loyalties, high-stakes conflict and
intense emotion.

⬥HARLEQUIN *Blaze*

Harlequin® Blaze stories sizzle with strong heroines and
irresistible heroes playing the game of modern love and lust.
They're fun, sexy and always steamy.

Be sure to check out our full selection of books
within each series every month!

www.Harlequin.com

HPASSION2016

HARLEQUIN®

A Romance FOR EVERY MOOD™

Love the Harlequin book you just read?

Your opinion matters.

Review this book on your favorite
book site, review site, blog or your own
social media properties and share
your opinion with other readers!

Be sure to connect with us at:
Harlequin.com/Newsletters
Facebook.com/HarlequinBooks
Twitter.com/HarlequinBooks